Destruction Via the Mirror Image

By
Stanley Pitchford

Stanley Pitchford

To Ms. Love,

Thanks for being a great coworker with me in the SSC, Lord knows how crazy things can get from the author!

10/30/08

P.O. Box 2535
Florissant, Mo 63033

Copyright ©2007 by Stanley Pitchford

All rights reserved. No part of this book may be reproduced or transmitted in any form by any means, electronic, mechanical, photocopy, recording or otherwise, without the consent of the publisher or the author, except as provided by USA copyright law.

Cover Designed by Karoz Norman
Manufactured in the United States of America

Library of Congress Control Number: 2007943853

ISBN 13: 9780979282379
ISBN 10: 0979282373

For information regarding discounts for bulk purchases, please contact Prioritybooks Publications at 1-314-741-6789 or rosbeav03@yahoo.com.
You can contact the author at: jabberstan@yahoo.com.

Table of Contents

Dedication	i
Introduction	1
Chapter One: The Take Off	19
Chapter Two: The Abilities of the Spaceship Hexapod	33
Chapter Three: A Soap Opera in Outer Space	49
Chapter Four: The Untouchable's Intro	83
Chapter Five: The Hexapod and The Untouchable's Collision	97
Chapter Six: Fatal Drama	117
Chapter Seven: The Baby Untouchable is Born	127
Chapter Eight: The Final Four	133
Chapter Nine: Tevie Versus The Untouchable	143
Chapter 10: It's Not Over Yet	153

Destruction Via the Mirror Image

By
Stanley Pitchford

PriorityBooks Publications
Florissant, Missouri

Dedication

This story is dedicated to Susan Pitchford, my grandmother, whom I love so much. She is the reason I wrote this book and without her, I do not know where I would be. This story is also dedicated to my brothers, Damon and Reginald Pitchford, my mother, Mary Pitchford, and my nieces, Marciay and Reje. Thank you all for believing in me more than I sometimes believe in myself.

    On my father's side, I send thank you's to my brothers and sisters – Jarron, Brandon, Jasmine and Brittany. There are so many people that I could mention here and even then I'm sure I'd miss someone, so to everyone who has made an impact on my life in one way or another, thank you from the bottom of my heart. And last but certainly not least, I thank God for this opportunity.

Introduction

Sometimes wanting to know too much can be delightful and sometimes it can be deadly. There are many of us who would not mind dying for something we love to do. Yet, most of us are not ready to die and, even if death were upon us from some illness, there would still be people who'd be angry just because they know that sooner or later they're going to die. They would probably be thinking they have nothing to lose.

But then, it could be some alien-like creature who scared you like the Boogeyman when you were three. Although you were scared of the monster, you still questioned how it got its features, and you were even curious about its ways and instincts. You wondered why it even crossed your path at that given time. And yet, you loved the thrill of being scared, because it gave you some sort of adrenaline rush. You never guessed that wanting to know so much more could actually turn into a disastrously bloody situation for a select group of people.

When humans think to become clever and exploratory, you would never think that a select group of people could die so quickly and without recognition. In real life, we, as humans, face the next day and it comes like a question mark. Clearly, no one ever knows when it will be his or her time to go and, yes, that includes me. You can wish that you were in a better place, maybe on a beach right before a wave comes through and catches the nice, fresh air blowing across where you're lying. You can read this story and it will

Introduction

copycat the dream you might have been having when you woke up as the rush came. The monster is gruesome and it does not care to be friendly.

Nevertheless, sometimes knowing just enough to succeed is all you need in life or in a dream. Why would you shoot for more if you already have enough? God said not to be greedy, anyhow. This could be why you are wrapped up in dreams that you cannot make disappear. And this could also be a dream that you need not know about.

This is the same idea with astronauts. Maybe there is stuff in outer space that we need not investigate or know about. Sometimes when you go too far you get bitten, anyway. The bites may come slow and then you wear yourself down with stress. You will never know how the whole story will unfold, but you are eager to see who will survive the bumpy road and you wonder if certain explorations are the right answer. Every move in life or in a dream is a choice, and sometimes you will sacrifice yourself in the consequences. Unfortunately, by the time you actually figure out the answer to a situation it is too late, and then you get annihilated before you have a chance to be successful and win. Of course, your thoughts mean nothing if you are a bloody corpse. Who can think when his or her head is cut off?

What is an exploration when it could mean fatal consequences? What is an adventure if you cannot come back to talk about your experiences? Whether you are alive or not, you care not to talk about the disaster. Yes, the story gets that gruesome and deadly. Who would ever know that something of a monster would intervene and destroy without reason? These are the questions that will hinder us all, even the critics, as we invoke on future reading into this story.

This story will remind you that sometimes you can explore something that you wish you had not. This story is meant to be suspenseful and to put a little fear into readers. So please be warned readers, this is just a book. The nature of this story will never happen the way you read it so do not take it seriously. The future can be a gold mine of opportunity, but it can also be the entrance to dangerous encounters that make us grateful for what the past had to offer. Let me, Tevron Jenkins, tell the story of how it all went down, carefully and cleverly.

It was the year 3055 and technology was racing beyond its old standards. Most of the world had gotten too lazy and this was bad. There were many jobs lost, yet many mechanical jobs born. Where people used to get up and cycle through the various television channels, using the knob on the television or wire pliers if the knob was lost or broken, a remote control made them even lazier. Where people used to sweat turning a can opener or twisting a certain something until its top came off, there were now devices that saved you from having to do anything. The devices did all the turning, sweating and working for you. I had gained sixty-two pounds since the invention of the remote alone. In grocery stores, four jobs had been eliminated and replaced with one cashier and one tech person, with the existence of the robotic tell-checkers that rang up food items. Can you imagine living like the Jetsons, riding around on hover boards or space cars in the atmosphere? Of course, this was the type

Introduction

of world we had approached and beyond.

As technology increased, all of the ailments that bothered humans before suddenly bothered them even more. They were so worried about technological advancements that some of them neglected their own health and well being. Technology was now able to help in cases of cancer, diabetes and other diseases and viruses that harmed many Americans. And of course, there were more ways to communicate than were needed.

Even the space frontier had interesting discoveries that were considered and explored by astronauts. Outer space was still an exploration tool for the Earth astronaut, which is what I chose to be. After careful observation, the world had collected the best twelve astronauts to fulfill the task of yet another voyage into outer space and I was one of those picked. We went in hopes of finding remnants of material we could investigate thoroughly. We were picked probably because we were each unique in our own way. Each one of us loved his or her work and we were sure to give a good report when we returned to Earth. All of us were honored to have an opportunity to go on a voyage. We went in hopes of finding something but it would be more than what we bargained for...

The story starts at the Warsan Avionics Center in Maryland, USA. Astronauts from all around the world, including me, were called to a big meeting. We talked amongst ourselves, trying to get to know each other and it got chaotic at times, because there had to have been hundreds of well-qualified astronauts in the place. Out of the many astronauts that came to the meeting only twelve of us were nominated to go on the voyage. Those twelve had to have charisma, attitude, faith, wisdom and, among other things, willpower to achieve the mission. After the Big Boss came to a decision on twelve people, we were all given information on each other.

First, I met Warsan Avionics supervisor, astronaut, and pilot, John Litzberger. He was forty-two and he had a wife and three kids back home in California. Also known as JL, he was around six feet tall, with an athletic build and a strategic mind. He played games like Clue, Tic-Tac-Toe and Battleship in his spare time. He made the final cut simply because the Warsan Avionics committee knew he had great potential. The Big Boss liked his charisma and courage. As I talked with JL, I thought he seemed like the kind of person who would charge at any obstacle and do whatever it took to be successful.

"So, since you made the final cut and I made the final cut, who do you think will be picked next?" I asked him.

"I do not know and I do not care. I just hope it is someone who will do their part in the job. That is all that matters," JL replied.

"I understand," I said calmly.

JL's vita was impressive. He had done well in school and he was considered a genius. He had always dreamed of becoming a great astronaut and he seemed like he would make a good leader. He had always admired the stars, the moon and the planets in our solar system and he was waiting for the day he could get up close with them. Though he was one of the oldest going on the voyage, he was fit from years of working out. It didn't take me long to come to the conclusion that his skill and thought processes were phenomenal.

The next person to be approved by the committee and assigned to the voyage did not always want to be an astronaut. In fact, he had originally wanted to be a biomedical engineer. His rap sheet said his name was Hayward Hidalgo, but he preferred to be called Hay-Hay. He was from South Korea, a place where people were constantly trying to understand more using advanced technological endeavors and ideas. I'd read somewhere that South Korean engineers actually played around with nuclear explosives and other dangerous explosive devices, in an effort to learn more about them.

Hay-Hay was a thirty-year-old computer expert who knew how to trigger devices for explosions. He was around five-six, with a mustache and a goatee, and he was not in the best physical shape. He told me that his wife, Pagella, had encouraged him to take this opportunity to be successful and that his two children could not wait for him to return home and tell them about what he had seen. Even though, Hay-Hay hadn't wanted to explore outer space until he was at least twenty-one, he wanted to retire as an astronaut, if possible.

"Congrats, congrats," I told him.

"Thank you kindly, sir," Hay-Hay replied. "I take it

you made the cut, also?"

"Yep."

I thought I knew why Hay-Hay had been picked for the voyage. He liked robots and computer technology, he could probably tell you anything about computers or computer technology, and he loved helping people. His fascination with math and science, and his confidence in his ideas and concepts was great, but he hadn't been expecting to be picked to go into outer space. He thought he had won the lottery, for sure.

Later, after I had eaten, I ran into Austin Ayoda, the highly intelligent Australian who happened to be the youngest of the twelve. To me, he was the babe of the voyage. He was twenty-one and eager to go on a voyage into outer space. He told me that he was a risk taker and that, when he was younger, he enjoyed games of risk and putting himself out there as a sacrifice. He felt he still had much to do and much energy to do it with.

"You are only as young as you feel," he said.

He had the mentality of a kid, always ready to explore something interesting. He was a single man and he did not mind getting bit by a bullet. I felt he would be fun to be around and I was glad he had been picked.

The next cadet picked, whom I saw later the same evening, was Carlos Lopez. He was a Spanish genius and, unlike Austin, he lived and died to be an astronaut. He told me that he had been built for this job and he had known the

Big Boss would pick him. At thirty-five, he was heavyset and fairly short, but good looking enough to attract very pretty women. He carried himself like he could do big things and he wasted no time telling me about some of the things he had already done. He had completed numerous internships and acquired many honors. Yet, he was hungry for more out of life.

"Life is about hard work and hustling to get to where you want to be," he said repetitively. He had a wife, three kids and a pit bulldog named Chase back home. Although Carlos was far from the most humble person I had ever met, I sensed that he had always been a hard worker and a caring provider for people.

He reminded me of my French boss, Paria Ponga, whom I had come to admire and love.

She was a foxy lady for a boss; five-eight and sexy, with a nice figure. She was a forty-year-old diva who had it going on.

When I finally caught up with her, I said, "You are so fine, lady. I just bet you got all the men in high school, huh?" She laughed in a blushing manner.

She treated all the other astronauts as if they were as highly ranked as she was. She was much like Hay-Hay, wanting the astronauts to assume their rightful duties whenever plausible, so that the voyage would be a success and nothing got chaotic. With all the turbulence and trauma one faced while being in outer space, she believed that astronauts should not grimace at all. All smiles and no cries, was her mentality. She was the best boss I had ever had in my life.

The next person I encountered after the meeting was Babatunde Alfa, the African who was also known as BA. He was a dark-skinned black man who loved mechanics. He was thirty-four, around five-nine, thin and slightly muscular. He shared with me that he had always wanted to see the stars up close and he was excited about getting a chance to do so. He was a rookie astronaut, willing to learn and utilize his mechanical skills whichever way he could.

He told me that he was anxious to give this a shot. He still could not believe he was picked. He had known what it was like not to have an opportunity, so whenever they presented themselves, he was determined to give his all and be successful.

When he was a kid he had lived off of corn and other vegetables. He could not afford many things because he had to be responsible with finances. He later found a job in mechanics and a short time later, he married a woman named Atoka. Together, they had five children.

And then there was NaHafa Toyo, a Japanese astronaut who was well known for her knowledge of avionics and electrical circuits. She was thirty-years-old and adventurous. She looked like she could be a supermodel and she certainly had the figure for it. Yet, she was single. Her boyfriend, she said, was the study of science. She had chosen this lifestyle because she said it kept her busy. As I listened to NaHafa talk about her life, I thought she was quiet and

Introduction

then I remembered how my granny used to tell me to always watch the quiet ones, because they might shock you one day.

After wrapping up my time with NaHafa, I ran into a cool, laid back guy named Aleandro Rodriguez, also known as A-Rod. Now how was that for a nickname? He was an astronomer who had always loved the space frontier and always wanted to be involved with it to make a difference. It seemed like he wanted to be a hero no matter what the cost. A-Rod was a handsome, slick, young twenty-four year old stud. He was an average size guy who seemed like a pretty boy. He told me that he was from Cuba, where he had studied astronomy. He had always enjoyed science related field trips as a kid, and constellations and how they came about in our galaxy. He'd always wanted to see the galaxy firsthand. Also, A-Rod loved fiestas and having fun, since all his family were professionals at throwing parties. He and his family had a good time at these parties. A-Rod knew how to dance and have a good time in front of others. It was just a typical thing for him to do to have fun.

He also studied science life forms and, for a third-year astronaut, he knew a great deal about things other than astronomy. He told me that there was a time for work and a time for play.

"Hey, I know I got to work in this life to make the dough, but I must get my boogie on, hombre," A-Rod said confidently.

And he always kept this perspective in mind. He was

single and always looking for a flame to keep him hot. Nevertheless, nothing would ever substitute or get in the way of his work. Although he was not eager or in a rush to get married, he told me that he was always searching for the right lady.

Later that same day, I ran into what seemed to be a sexy, slut in my view- Safoya Sarayova, the Slavic. She was the robotics queen of the voyage and she knew many other things, as well. She was a nice lady but she had the personality of a gerbil. I realized this by the way she carried herself. She had the type of body that any man would find attractive and try to take advantage of. She was a hot twenty-four year old, who was attractive in her own style and in her own way. She looked professional, but she had other characteristics later to be revealed. She had a nice, flexible physique that was definitely approachable to any man, including me. She was really something to see. She knew she was a breath of fresh air, the way she strutted with such confidence when she approached me. Also, she was great with computer technology and she knew how to fix things. She really shocked me with what she said she was capable of doing. She was young with all of this talent and knowledge and single, too.

I still thought about the fact that she did not have a man. She claimed to have had bad luck with men, so she loved her work instead. She was sure her work could be a challenge at times, but it would not ever let her down.

She had been an astronaut since she was nineteen and she learned new things every year. She hoped the voyage was a success and that it could be something for her to tell future generations and siblings. She was so conceited about her work while she was in school that she never really gave boys a chance to talk to her. She was conceited and confident about her way of life, sure enough. She could be flashy, but not too much, as if to tease anybody. Safoya and I would chitchat like I was interviewing her, but I was really just getting to know her.

"Why are you questioning me so much? Like you are the detective and I need an alibi?" she uttered.

"I just want to get to know my coworkers on the ship and their habits, so I know what to expect," I answered quickly.

"What you do not know, you need to find out about, honey, but do not ask me directly. I am not that type of lady!" she proclaimed.

It seemed that everybody who made the voyage who was not from America spoke good English and pronounced words and syllables well. Safoya did this and was quite fine with it, too. I admit she was probably the finest lady on the ship but I knew she already knew that.

And then there was me, Tevron Jenkins, the American from the ghetto slums of Los Angeles, California. The other American who'd had a complicated journey in life. I'd had problems in my past, but I had been blessed like others.

Most people called me Tevie. I was a twenty-eight year old African-American male, with courage and the ability to think clearly. I was no psychic, but I did have great visions of things that might occur if I did not make the right decisions. I was a six-foot tall hustler type guy, who wore loose clothing, because I was determined to be comfortable. And I was determined to be successful no matter how much struggle and trouble I had to go through, because to me I had nothing to lose except my life. I did whatever it took to achieve a goal or mission.

In my life, I'd had four children by two different women and I was married to one of the women. I had trouble with education at first because my concentration was bad, but then I finally finished school with an emphasis in biomedical engineering. Also, I managed to learn other technological aspects, as well. I loved math and always thought it would never fail me. I wanted to be the problem solver and the one who knew he could break the yolk. I would try to do more great things to make up for the bad things I had put myself through. One's life was not marked by how many things one did, but it seemed to me that it always helped.

I could be a hacker, if need be, if it benefited things in a good way. I was good with a computer and, although I was not into mechanics, I could fix things if pressured in the moment.

Things did not work out with my first baby's mother, because she did not believe in my dreams. She literally shot down my success and aspirations like I could be nothing but some lazy black man who was struggling all the time. She would say things like she thought she saw right through me, but really she did not know me. She always talked me down, saying, "You will never have anything to show, being

Introduction

an astronaut. Those people leave this planet and sometimes do not come back. Are you trying to get a Purple Heart or something? What is with you?"

Of course, I stood my ground firmly like a man would. I remembered that she read a lot of stories about the history of the Columbia disaster that left shrapnel falling out of the air across the nation years ago. Furthermore, she thought I was not fit to be an astronaut. She thought I should be a gym teacher or a bodybuilder or maybe get a job in computer technology. She wanted me to get a job close to home, doing something else. She knew I had a great mind that could be useful for other things and she knew I was in shape, too.

Nevertheless, I loved to explore. In fact, I would look at the stars with my dad at night and watch them glow. My mom and dad would pick me up to see the stars when I was little. But I would not tell her these things because I doubt she cared. I wanted to be somebody big, someone who would leave a mark that would be remembered by others for a long time.

Just like A-Rod, I was into science fiction and horror. As a child, I liked watching movies like Robocop and Friday the 13th. Also, in my leisure time, I loved to do karate, to release some stress. I was a very active astronaut who loved to be alert and aware of things. This being my rookie astronaut voyage, it was a great experience for me. But enough about me.

Let us not forget about Manuel "Manny" Pearson, the New Yorker who was the oldest astronaut on the voyage.

He was from The Bronx, New York, USA. He was a muscular guy who was medium in height and size. He was a forty-two year old African-American male who was excited to be picked for the voyage. He told his friends to call him "Brother Man" as a nickname, but I thought "Manny" was better. He was a hip guy, but you could not tell directly. He was a sixth year astronaut and pilot. He told me many things about outer space. When I met up with Manny, he gave me the history of astronauts.

"Astronauts have come a long way in their discoveries of new life forms. So much technology is available to us now than there ever was in the past."

"Do you think there are life forms on all the planets of the solar system?" I questioned him.

"I do not know," Manny responded.

Manny loved the engineering side of things. Back home, when he was younger, he enjoyed watching his father fix cars around the house. Later, Manny was taught everything there was to know about nursing a car back to health. He remembered his dad always telling him, "A car is like a moving house, unless you want to pay someone to fix things that go wrong, you're going to have to learn about your ride so you can take care of it."

He would get through high school and then earn masters degrees in electrical and mechanical engineering. Shortly thereafter, he got married and he now had five kids, two of whom wanted to be astronauts like him. His kids were proud of him and they loved talking to him about outer space. After he retired he wanted to be a representative for youngsters who were interested in being astronauts or space pilots. He loved helping out the next man, because this made him feel really good and he treated the younger astronauts like they were his own kids. He was much like Paria, who wished that everybody would assume their rank and position and follow it. This was supposed to be a fun and exciting adventure, he perceived, and as long as the exploration was fun, everybody would be happy and the voyage would go that much smoother.

Finally, there was Yao Ying, the Chinese expert who was a mechanical wizard. She also knew about robotics and avionics. I ran into her in the hallway after the Big Boss had made his picks. I walked toward her to greet her, congratulate her, and ask her questions. She told me she was twenty-six years old with much experience at being a skilled astronaut. She could teach others a thing or two about computers and electronics, as well. As a little girl in China, she played with robotic toys and enjoyed them. She was a shy girl who really did not like to make many friends.

"I was only this way because, as I was growing up, my parents were pretty strict on me. But I think it paid off," Yao uttered. "Also, being shy helps out a lot because your peers do not know if you are smart or dumb," she added. "Surely, you have heard this wisdom before: 'It's the quiet and shy ones you've got to watch'?" For a Chinese lady, her English was almost as good as mine was, if not better. And she had a sexy voice, but it was almost like she did not want to show it while she was talking to me. She was mainly focused on the voyage and nothing else.

She was best at the mechanical side of things, since she was good with her hands. She was a cute Chinese gal who was about five-three, and she could model because she had a welcoming smile and physique. She knew a little about martial arts, also. But to her, martial arts served as a discipline, not as a weapon, unless it was needed.

This single girl made things by hand. She made potholders, wreaths and knitted clothing. She said she cooked delicious Chinese dishes, also. Just looking at her, I knew the voyage committee had been fascinated by her personality, among other things, and this was why she had made the final cut as a member of the voyage crew.

After we were all picked, we sat in the Green Marble Room, which was a popular room for meetings of high officials. Also, this would be the communications center where the astronauts would be able to give and get information about progress on the voyage. The Big Boss resided there and big decisions were decided in that particular room. The center's technology was in abundance. They had all the high-tech, state of the art paraphernalia to make the voyage a success.

The Center was huge, about the size of five football fields, and the people there exchanged information with other countries across the world. The fifty stations in the center were interconnected with other major stations around the world. It was like a circuit of communication all around the world. There were one hundred substations just to operate

Introduction

and monitor the voyage itself. The Warsan satellite, located toward the south, served as a buffer to get the location of the people on the voyage. The Center had the power to authorize missile attacks, if need be. In addition, the first captain had this power, as well. First Captain Ponga would never override the Avionics Center's demands unless she had no other choice and she felt it was the only answer.

So we were the selected members that would form the BASIC 12, or the company throughout this story. Of course, we had only one task to fulfill, to stay true to the voyage and seek new and interesting phenomena, while having fun in outer space. The Warsan Center would monitor the movement of our spacecraft via radar for as long as their technology allowed it. Now that everybody had been picked, we were sure to party and celebrate next.

Chapter One:
The Take Off

Three nights before take-off, the astronauts gathered and partied. There was such harmony in the room as we met and greeted one another. This was a time for all of the astronauts to get acquainted with each other and our families.

"Well this is it. Are you ready, soldier? I mean, cadet astronaut?" Manny asked me.

"I was born ready. Always alert and thinking about the whole situation, man," I replied.

Yao came over to me, gave me a hug for good luck and then asked, "Would you like some Chinese food later?"

"Nah, I mean, no thanks. I will just eat what my wife fixed me."

At the time, life did not seem so clear to me. I surely thought I was making all the right moves. Things definitely got better after my break-up with my first child's mother, Latoya. But I still felt like I did not understand my place in life. I felt like I was passing through time and not really understanding who I was or how lucky I could be. I never even thought of how dangerous things could get for me or anyone else and I never really understood how lucky one was to be alive.

I was daydreaming all of this before I approached the hall for the party. They really had the place looking nice at every angle, with nice chandeliers and drapes hanging from

Chapter 1

the ceiling. There was much liquor to drink and nicotine to smoke. Of course, I really did not like to drink or smoke and this bothered some but not others.

"What do you do to get stress off of you?" A-Rod asked.

"I could surely exercise, meditate, or write rhymes to get rid of any negative vibes," I answered. "I could go boxing like BA does."

You could surely drink thoughts of any problems away with all the stuff they had. They had nice brands of wines and wine pills that were programmed with a good percentage of alcohol. You could get the dissolving pill or you could get it in a glass. Either way, if any person wanted to get something to drink, their satisfaction was guaranteed and the party was "off the chain."

There were so many cultures at the party and so many dances were being taught by people from countries all across the world. It seemed like there was so much to do; yet there was so little time. Everybody was sure to get their groove on that night. Carlos danced the salsa and A-Rod did the same. They drank to their hearts content. "Gulp, gulp," A-Rod's throat throttled as he took a drink from the wineglass in his hand. Yao brought some Chinese checkers and games for her and JL to play. She won most of the games at first, but as the night wore on JL started to win.

While they were playing, Manny and me drank liquor and smoked cigars. "Somebody paid for us to get drunk during our last days on earth for a while," I told him.

"We got some voyage to go on soon, eh?" Manny said, puffing a cigar. "I just think about how nice the place looks and how much trouble they went through just to make sure we got sent away knowing how great these three days were."

"But it is a real test," I added. Although I do not really drink, I got a little tipsy myself, but it was a party. I knew I was not going to drive or do anything constructive where I could get into trouble, so it was alright.

Safoya, NaHafa and BA danced African dances shown by BA and his family.

"Y'all look mighty nice with those sexy dance moves."

"Hey, do you think you can do any better? Come on, show us what you got, Tevie boy!" Safoya and NaHafa replied.

"I could show you a thing or two, if you like, Tevie," BA uttered.

"Nah, I am good. Ladies always out do me in dancing, so I will spare y'all my embarrassment," I said rapidly.

All of this was brought on because BA used to belong to a tribe back in Africa. He learned how to dance through bodily expression, not just music. Dancing to music was almost like yoga and meditation combined. When he moved it was almost like he was moving with the rhythm, the music and the air in the room. You could tell he had too much prac-

Chapter 1

tice at these dances because it seemed like he had mastered them. I could see Safoya staring at BA's shape while he was doing those dances so smoothly, moving his arms. She gazed at his movements as if she was attracted to them.

Safoya asked, "What's that? The Bombatta or what?"

"I cannot say I do not like it but what is it called?" BA answered. "It was just something I made up, and just moved with the music. See madam, you must listen to the beat and really feel the music, as if it is sending messages through your skin."

I was laughing at their dance moves, but for some reason, I started to like it. Now that was weird to think about. How could I shoot down something and then turn around and like it? "Hey let me join this wild dancing. It seems kind of dirty," I added.

Paria and Hay-Hay sat back and relaxed on nice sofas and sipped club soda. "Are you really relaxed like I am Hay-Hay?" Paria said.

"Well, uh, maybe too relaxed in these deep laid back lazy-boy seats," Hay-Hay responded.

Austin Ayoda was not so much of a party guy, but he would still get his groove on later. Austin was one of those astronauts who wanted to get everything over with so he could get back home. He was really seeking the astronaut duty at hand, and one could definitely depend on that from him because that is all he cared about. Later, Austin shocked me with the moves he was doing on the dance floor.

"Hey, did you see BA earlier?" I questioned. "You seem like him when you dance." I wondered if those were Australian rituals or something. "Hey let me in on the secret," I laughed. "If you really cannot dance just admit it, and there are people here that will teach you."

Carlos told A-Rod, "Do you know how to salsa?"

A-Rod answered, "Fool, what is your problem? Bring it on! I am an A+ in this. I will cha-cha you out of your shoes man!" A-Rod boasted. "The drinks were never better too, but I am just satisfied with service and a smile. I see this party got started off right, no doubt. Let us fiesta!"

But Yao spoke again. "Anyone for some Chinese games with me and JL?" JL replied, "Well I do not know about the rest of the company, but winning at Chinese games always makes me a great thinker."

I thought he was right about the thinking part. When I was younger Chinese games did make me think better and smarter. It would seem to the rest of the company that partying and dance was more interesting than playing Chinese games with Yao.

Paria would go from furniture to furniture testing the comfort of each piece "I never knew furniture could be this soft and comfortable," she said to herself.

Also, the astronauts' kids were altogether in a room by themselves, getting to know one another for the next

Chapter 1

three days. It was so noisy in there at times because everybody was playing some type of game or something. They had far more advanced systems for kids to play, to stimulate their minds. They introduced themselves to each other and immediately started to enjoy each other's company. There had to be at least 60 or 70 people in the room. It was hard to believe that they managed in that little area.

Some kids would walk around in astronaut suits, pretending to be in outer space. Some would pretend to be aliens. There was much dancing, singing and celebrating for them, as well, because families knew that they would not see each other for a while.

That night we never forgot. It resided in my heart throughout the whole story. The next morning, it was like a disaster throughout the whole area, since there was so much cleaning up to do. There were beer bottles all over the floor, trash flooding the hallways, cigarette butts on the ground, and we would not get to the cleaning up until later. We slept like we had partied forever and forever and were so tired. Nevertheless, everybody partied again later the next evening.

Lunchtime came and everybody gathered around a huge rectangular table in the hall, as if it were some royal meeting or conference. We played more icebreaker games and other games like dodge ball, two-hand touch football, baseball, basketball, and tennis. They made the whole event look like a family reunion, like relatives who had not seen each other in ages.

The second night came rapidly and the fun never stopped. The adults played more games and drank whatever they felt in the mood for drinking. The kids went on hay rides at night and to theme parks during the day. The second night was so special, in that some people actually got to know each other a little bit better. The gathering of the whole reunion took place in a city located near Maryland.

A-Rod and Safoya knew each other a little bit better than expected. They mingled together that night. A-Rod said, "Let me take a picture of this smile, because I do not know if I will see it again."

Safoya answered, "Is that the best line you got, sir?"

He replied, "I got more, but I do not want to waste your time and mine with all those other ones." She laughed.

Of course, one thing led to another and fireworks would go off that night for them, I assumed. I saw a vibe between them at the party, so I knew things would take off shortly after that.

"You want to kiss me so badly, don't you, sweetheart?" Safoya whispered.

"Yes, yes, yes, I would like to very much," A-Rod said, nervously shaking. Safoya was overwhelmed by the motives and actions of A-Rod that they became lovers that night, but the commitment was kept a secret at the time. They kissed each other in a closed closet area, away from all the action.

Chapter 1

"Let us take it nice and slow," Safoya added. "You want to treat this as a one night stand?"

"No one will ever know," A-Rod replied.

Safoya replied, "We can treat this however you want and that is the truth."

It seemed that they did not want the rest of the astronauts to know about their rendezvous. Safoya had on this nice formal wear dress, looking so gorgeous, and A-Rod had on this black suit with black slacks, looking so handsome. Even though his personality made him look like he should be wearing a Hawaiian shirt with Docker shorts, he still looked good in formal attire. Nevertheless, it would look bad for them if everybody knew their special secret.

In addition, NaHafa flirted with A-Rod from time to time and he began to notice her. It was like she was a wild cat on the prowl, purring all over A-Rod at times at the party.

"I guess age is nothing but a number in her mind," I thought to myself. I must admit, it was going to be pretty lonely being in a spaceship with only twelve people after a while, so that was why she acted the way she did, I thought. So much joy and fun happened in the first two nights. Okay, for some maybe too much fun, yet it seemed that they ran out of things to do for the third day, since they did so much during the first two.

* * * *

The following morning the voyage company had

many choices for breakfast, including eggs, bacon, sausage, pancakes, hash browns, grits, or oatmeal, and waffles even, with a choice of orange juice or milk. Cereal was on the menu also, but it was a meal in a pill that you could take and it filled you up and excited your taste buds, as well. The pill had a little spark that also refreshed your breath, so that your breath would not smell like milk. Technology was so advanced and humans proved to be lazier as time kept racing. Anyway, the wives, kids, relatives and friends of the company went back to the theme park to get on rides and have more fun. It was a fun filled day and people were merry, as if it was their last days on Earth.

Later that day, me and the rest of the company had a brief meeting. The company, or the BASIC 12, which was what we were called as a nickname, discussed the instructions for take off and preparations. The Big Boss called via satellite to wish us good luck on the voyage and tell us to have a safe trip, indeed. "I expect everything to go smoothly, my fellow cadets," the Big Boss uttered quickly.

"I am so excited about everything," Hay-Hay shouted.

"I feel you, homes. I am too," said A-Rod.

I was just as excited as everybody else and eager to get everything rolling. I just had bad feelings and thoughts that something bad would happen down the road. This meeting was mandatory for the company only but somehow, some of the company's relatives managed to crash the meeting. This day seemed long since we did not do much at all except

Chapter 1

laugh and joke about things and smile more. The jokes I told only made me think about the finer things in life, so I would not be so stressed out thinking about how far away from my family and close friends I would be. We all tried not to think about that and did things that never reflected that.

Later that day, each of the company's spouses had a meeting and played grown-up games like Bingo, and discussed the future of being without their counterparts.

And Paria had another meeting to bring what we were dodging to our attention and raise our confidence at the same time. "It is going to take some getting used to, huh? Being without your wife or your husband for a while," Paria preached. "But we need to think about the mission and keep the energy there at all times once we hit outer space. "I have been through this kind of drama before on previous voyages and it takes some getting used to," Paria added.

Each single astronaut had conversations with each other that afternoon. They really had no family to go back home to, so the company was our family, because we are all in this voyage together. Everybody gathered and played more games until late night. It seemed like a lighter night in partying than the other two though. The kids and teenagers played video games, circus type games to win candy, and the older kids and adults played card games like Dominoes and Spades. Others played games like Truth or Dare. Of course, this was supposed to be the final night before the launch and take-off, but it seemed like just another family reunion that none of the company would ever forget. It seemed like we played Truth or Dare all night and the limits were expanded to anything goes, but by that time there were only a few people left and we decided to just cut and quit.

It was hard to go to sleep that night. I tossed and turned in my bed, adrenaline trembling, since I knew the next day the launch would take place. I was so nervous. I had butterflies and all kinds of dreams about what might happen. Manny and I kept playing Spades and Dominoes.

"Give me fifteen points, homey."

As Manny slapped the dominoes hard against the table, I replied, "I will definitely be sending you to the bone yard, so get ready, playa! Now we are playing a real man's game now, you hear me?"

Yao and John kept playing Chinese Checkers since JL knew that not many people were interested in Yao's games. Then everybody finally went to sleep very late. And all was quiet shortly after two in the morning.

* * * *

Select people woke up early to fix breakfast or brunch, since they knew it would be their last meal on Earth with their families for a while. This was the first meal they did not eat as a group in unison. It seemed like the day started out gloomy, like a tired rain that lasted all day. Some people slept like they did not want the day to start because they knew it was launch day.

We all got together for one more big event, but this was our last one together as a whole. This final event was a

Chapter 1

trip to the zoo. There were so many animals at the zoo, and it was nice to see everybody there. It made me feel proud to see everybody in attendance. Some of us took pictures with the animals, reminding them that it marked the last time they were on Earth with their fellow astronauts before the voyage. I actually took a shot of me next to an elephant. We all had a big lunch together at the zoo and we talked and giggled, but that would soon be the last time everybody ate together as a whole.

Finally, they all left the zoo, and everybody headed back to their appropriate hotels and lodging to make sure each of the BASIC 12 had packed efficiently for launch. In addition, the company's relatives had to get back to their rightful places, as well, to pack and leave for their own homes. Moreover, husbands kissed wives and kids were in tears, knowing that he or she would not see their parent for a while. So much crying and emotional feeling was felt. This gathering lasted three hours, since it was so heart-felt, like someone very important had died or something. I cried on this day, and most of the company did, also. My four kids wished me well and they understood my situation because I told them beforehand, and I was on my way. The company bus pulled up, and then more tears poured out of the kids and spouse's eyes, like it was really going to happen. Saying goodbye was about the hardest thing to do for everybody.

Each person of the company was allowed ten minutes to get as many hugs and kisses from as many people as they could, and then he or she went to board the bus. Of course, this would take two or three hours at least, but it was well worth it. Of course, kids hugged and did not want to let go. They used the rest of the minutes to get to the Warsan Center for Avionics so that the BASIC 12 could settle in on the spaceship. Of course, later in the afternoon, the launch took place. In addition, many of the company's relatives and friends raced to the Avionics center to wave goodbye one last time.

Avionics center workers had the BASIC 12's equipment packed in well. They were ready for the launch to start. The counter on the spaceship started counting down from 90 minutes. Each of the BASIC 12 company got into their positions, checking the equipment to make sure everything worked efficiently and effectively. While the time was moving, we packed more junk food and sofas, and other materials that would make our trip even more comfortable.

"Well, this is it, you ready, homes!" A-Rod spoke to me.

"I was born ready," I answered quickly.

"I prayed about it enough," Manny added.

"Everything will be okay, just keep thinking positive you guys," Paria yelled.

We all counted together and when we got to ten, I said, "Here we go, ten, nine, eight, seven, six, five, four, three, two, one, LIFT OFF! The countdown had come and gone, and the take-off started in the newly named spaceship, which was...

Chapter Two:
The Abilities of the Spaceship Hexapod

Yes, more tears came as the spaceship began its take-off, and family and friends waved in honor of us. We breached the Earth's atmosphere and then met up with the network communications satellite. We sizzled into the air with no hesitation. We saw the shape of the Earth go from a big round sphere to a small blue stress ball. Later, it appeared as a speck of something as we got farther away from it. The moon seemed too close in view at first, like it was pulling us toward it. Some of the group had never seen it up close before. We all gazed at how nice the solar system looked.

"This seems like a once in a lifetime thing, homes. Look!" A-Rod said.

"It is surely a nice view every time I see it," Manny uttered.

While the rest of the BASIC 12 admired space, I got a little home sick, but I would soon get better and used to the whole thing. I never thought for one second that this could actually happen to me. And maybe it was because I thought something bad might happen that I felt this way.

"Is everything okay, comrade?" Manny spoke close by.

"I am fine. I will be okay, it will just take some time to get used to," I replied. "I know I am stronger than this," I

Chapter 2

thought to myself.

Paria spoke, "Tevie, everything will be alright once you get used to the company and this wonderful spaceship. We are living better than Star Trek up in this mutha."

"She's right, homie. You need to vibe the greatness you're in right now. Let us live it up while we are worthy," Manny added.

Now, we were aboard the best spaceship ever designed by labor to float in outer space. This spaceship was named Hexapod. It was given the name because it had six battle pod stations that could perform equal duties. Each battle station had two substations, which fitted the BASIC 12 or the company. The Hexapod had legs at each station, too.

"Hey Tevie, are you talking to yourself, dude?" JL uttered.

"Nah, just thinking out loud about the awesomeness of the spaceship we are on," I replied. JL walked away from me down a corridor.

Right now the legs of the ship were folded up in the lower part of the ship. If the spaceship ever had to land again, it landed on all six legs. It was really weird because we took off like a rocket, but we could land better than an airplane. The spaceship had a force field shield on reserve for invaders. It could launch missile attacks, if need be. The missiles were custom-made to be nearly perfect, with little deficiency. The Hexapod also had the capability to zoom into hyperspace to evade any unwanted company.

There were many nice new features installed by Warsaw Industries, the makers of the spaceship. The ship tracked substances light-years away. It had better than state-of-the-art technology. The industry knew the materials and additions to the spaceship proved to be flawless, and that notion was based on how great the ship looked. The Hexapod could spin around quickly and maneuver, if attacked. It also had two back-up primary spaceships for emergency evacuations on either side of the lower level that could go relatively fast like the Hexapod. .

The spaceship's quarters were designed as if the spaceship was a royal mansion. "It's like a castle in outer space," I murmured to myself. It had nice, comfortable chairs that seemed lavishly fit for a prince or princess.

The Warsan Avionics Committee members had laid out the wardrobe for the BASIC 12. Our spaceship gear was almost fireproof. The women had elegant clothes to wear, nice after seven dresses and lingerie that would seem attractive on them and fit their shapes. The guys had tuxedos and handsome space attire that made us look like we were going to the Oscars to win Academy Awards. We had our own clothing that we had packed for the trip, but the center gave us more than enough to survive for years.

The rations were in abundance of what we needed and the food was healthy, so that we could be vital and strong. In other words, we had too much to eat. There were numerous first aid kits and security materials throughout the spaceship, too.

Chapter 2

It was like a dream vacation in the air that would never end. There was nothing you could mention that the ship did not have. I could not understand why I even got homesick at that point. The ship was over-prepared for only twelve people.

There were many leisure things to do on the ship, as well. There was a gym and poolroom, a casino and an engine smelting room. There were three main floors. The walls were covered with rugs for insulation. There was also a spa and a sauna and all these things were made in good taste. There were vending machines just about everywhere you went, if you wanted chips, cookies, soda and other kinds of junk to eat. There were also healthier snack vending machines, with vitamin pills in them. Most of the machines were located near the kitchen or by the gym. The spaceship gave us more stress-free relaxation than we actually needed at any one time. "I do not think we had this much opportunity at home!" I said to myself.

Later, while in outer space, we had a mandatory meeting. Paria Ponga spoke, "Hello my fellow cadets, I hope your trip is as exciting as mine is so far. I am the initial boss of the ship," she said. "Let me tell you how the rank will go and who will be in charge. Please believe me when I say this, I do not like to discipline anyone, really. But if you are out of line and not on task, well what do you think a sister is supposed to do? I am the first leader, then there is Commanding Officer Carlos Lopez. Then Captain John Litzberger. After him, leadership will be placed in rank order according to the number of years as an astronaut. We feel that seniority with astronauts is in experience and it is important to the mission," she uttered. "The Big Boss at Warsan Center gave me this authority. I am truly a nice woman, but I can get ugly if you push the wrong buttons. I am too nice to my own kids, almost like we are brothers and sisters or close friends, on the same level or something." She told us this with such admiration and smiled. Then she told us that she was glad everybody had fun in those three days before the launch. "Those days were so important for two reasons. It is never certain if we will make it back together and it gives our relatives and friends something to hold on to while we are not next to them for some days. Plus, we wanted to make those three days the most memorable as possible for our families and friends, and I think we did that so well. The mission in this voyage is to seek new activity and technological support, and search new information. I know that does not seem like a good reason for the situations that could happen, but let us be confident and stay positive on the assignment from the Big Boss. Please be reminded that we may not find anything, but it will have been a nice voyage. Plus, we get to enjoy all the nice advantages this ship has and there are many. I wish everybody the best in this voyage, and the best thing for all of us to do now is have fun and remember that we are all in this together."

She went on. "We are only twelve people, so the least we can do is be kind to one another and help each other whenever needed. I thank you for allowing me to be your leader in the voyage. I will let the next leader in charge speak," said Commander Ponga.

Chapter 2

And then Carlos Lopez spoke. "Hello company, how is everybody?" Everyone responded that we were fine. "Well, I am glad to be second in command, to help out the other ten people. I have a cool personality, as you will soon realize, but I can get hard on people at times, as well. When I do, it is out of the goodness of my heart, trust me. I am at least a moral man. I believe every human is at least moral and knows what is right and what is wrong. If you are wrong, you will hear from me about it. With all of that said, I love to have fun, as many of you know from the three-day gathering. I would just advise you to be on your best behavior, by respecting your position and your fellow cadets as astronauts. You should also find ways to have fun, since there are plenty of things this ship has to offer. You can have robots serve you meals and tuck you in at night. That is really awesome. I like the robotic masseuse we have on the ship. I think they made this ship specifically for lazy people, who do not have the energy to wash a dish, so they have dishwashing robots. If we're not too careful we might go back home overweight, so pull some weight around here so you do not become a potato. There are so many video games and other relaxing things to do that it's endless. I am truly a fighter for universal peace, so we must work toward that goal. I like voyages because they are good ways to preserve peace. I love the many attributes to the Hexapod, which makes me enjoy this voyage even more. Remember the voyage was designed to find new life or take note of new discoveries we have not yet seen before or otherwise. We all want to make this voyage a success and not a failure," he said. "And now I call John to the podium."

John spoke. "From here on out call me JL, and that goes for every cadet under my rank. If Carlos and Paria want to call me John, well then okay, I will accept that. As your flight supervisor and advice captain, I will give the best solution I can give to anything related to science and technology. I am really no critical thinker, but I do my best in the realm of science. I am really pleased to be aboard this ship. I am so glad that they have a gym. Maybe there is a chance that we will not be potatoes when we get back. Paria's advice to all of us was about having fun while we can on this ship. We are all in this thing together and no one can take that away from us twelve. Now I will let the next in command under me speak," JL said.

And Hayward Hildalgo spoke. "What is going on company?" The rest of the company yelled, "Hey Hay-Hay," in response. From then on, Hay-Hay replied, "I am honored to be nominated fourth in command, but I hate bossing people. I just like the fact that people do whatever job they are qualified to do. I should not have to tell people to do things that they are already supposed to have done already. I should not have to spoon feed people. I do not look at the fact that I have been an astronaut since a teenager, I look at the new things that we must encounter. I feel that you cannot put a rookie into an all veterans match and expect him or her to prosper effectively. I try to find a way to acknowledge these things and give good challenges for these things. We should have fun in all the great things that the ship has to offer. In addition, we must remember why we are here. Just think about it, we were twelve picked out of the whole world and so many other people could be in our shoes. So that by itself

Chapter 2

must mean something," Hay-Hay said to us. "Nevertheless, we must represent the world and this is a great honor to consider as an astronaut. This rank and ribbon on our uniforms does not mean a thing if we do not represent correctly. I hate to be so stuck up about the whole thing, but this meeting was so important to have, so that the ground rules get laid out for everybody under me to understand clearly. It is so important for all of us to intercommunicate as a team. No matter what differences we may encounter with each other, we all must still help each other, regardless," Hay-Hay explained sincerely.

Yao Ying spoke. "Hello all, I just want to enjoy our voyage, and I am looking forward to this most memorable experience. I do not really say much, I just do much observation. I am also glad we called this meeting again on the ship as the BASIC 12, or the Company. I know we left our real family on Earth, but we are family now on this ship. It will be this way until we get back home. But to me, it will always be this way, because we are all cadets of survival. It is very important we all understand that first. In addition, we have to remember that, while in the midst of a voyage such as this, if you are looking for a good Chinese dish to eat, you need to let me know because I have some good recipes on hand. I know everybody has had some chop suey, but not my kind.

"Wow, we actually can get Chinese in outer space. Cool," I thought.

She continued, "I can get really inventive with the rice and much more too. I am famous for a special fried rice dish, of course." Yao continued to boast about her Chinese food skills and how pleased she was to be on the voyage.

Manny spoke. "Hey, will we have to pay for that rice?"

Yao answered, "Food is money and the money will get me more food."

Manny replied, "Show you're right, madam. It is a business, just like everywhere back home."

Later Manny spoke again. "What's new, fellow cadets? I think it is mandatory that everybody must have fun while being on this ship. However, if we have too much fun, it can easily distract the truth of what we are trying to locate in this mission. For example, the Hexapod has eight different types of saunas, depending on skin type and how hot you want things. I am willing to try every one. It could be sauna type for hot, warm, or whatever. At the same time, we have to be aware of suspicious activity that may possibly jeopardize us all. Remember, it is only us twelve and no one else. Never act like you can figure out everything. Always find help in time of need by radioing someone, because two heads are always better than one. So being alert is important, but you can still enjoy the Hexapod, as well. Please, by all means, take advantage of all the various opportunities the Hexapod has. One may never get a chance like this ever again in a lifetime. We did it; we got our winning lottery ticket into outer space. I will now allow someone else to speak at this time."

Safoya Sarayova spoke, "Hello all. I am having so

Chapter 2

much fun so far on this spaceship. I think it is so exciting to be a fellow member. I love to play tennis and swim and have fun, so I will fall in love with the gymnasium that they have on the ship. I love to keep my fine, sexy shape fit. So I will be in the weight room if you need me in the near future. I would hate my description to be characterized as fat. If anyone said I was fat the next few seconds you might see me in that weight room pumping something or running on a treadmill. Anyway, I did not think a ship could hold such gymnasiums and still function as well as it does. Imagine, state-of-the-art equipment on a spaceship. This is truly wonderful. Although I am not the game-playing type, I may have to adopt that craft, since only eleven other people will surround me. I will have to get used to all. So much for secrets I guess. I got my wish, since I am in outer space just as I wanted, but did not know I would be seventh in command on such a colossal spaceship. I am honored to have this, and I am a cadet just like anyone else. I am not a prideful person, yet I am still reaching success. In addition, I like the beauty salon and cosmetic sections of the ship. I am trying to get some type of spaceship hair-do that will suit me and that others will like."

I sighed. "Geez, just like a woman," I thought to myself.

"I can look beautiful for somebody if I want, especially with all the supplies that they have on this ship. This Hexapod is unbelievable. With so many technological advancements and changes, they have upgraded spaceships to have more than what the average human needs to be successful. I hope we do not get lazy with all of this help. I will not worry. I refuse to allow myself to get fat and all bent out of shape. With that said, I will never go without anything much."

I assumed Safoya was thinking, "I will have to do something to get things cooking around here."

And then Aleandro Rodriguez spoke. "Wassup company? Well, if I get the commanding rank I am shocked because everybody knows I am the class clown. But I know everybody will be on their best behavior, since the three-day gathering was such a success. Now, it is about time to get down to business on this voyage and have a great time at the same time. I love the space frontier and everything about its originality. I could not wait to see the milky-way galaxy. I am a lover of this life and I will do anything to keep advances in outer space in existence. Astrology and astronomy are like my closest friends. I love to see new creations and life in our galaxy. I just love to explore new things. I am thrilled to see anything that seems odd to the naked eye. It really fascinates me. Even the Hexapod, with the best equipment, it can key in specifically on one aspect of something. That in itself is amazing!" he shouted to the rest of the company. "We have surely come a long way in technological advancements. I am delighted to help in any way I can to help make this voyage a successful one. So much time and effort was put into the whole extravaganza. Plus, I want this to be the most memorable time I've ever had with people. Years ago, the spaceship Electrocron, the spaceship before the Hexapod, was advanced, but not nearly

Chapter 2

as advanced as the Hexapod is."

In the last voyage, he was a cadet captain leader on that spaceship. Although he did not find anything, it was a nice trip to get to know new people from all over the world. He loved to interact with different people and understand their cultural ways of living. He was sure that this would be the same experience. I remember the Electrocron, which had too many electrical deficiencies that would short circuit from time to time. The Hexapod was capable of doing things that impressed me as an astronaut. As a matter of fact, as I saw the Hexapod in its great setup, it made me feel absolutely proud to be an astronaut and part of the company.

Sooner or later, we all got a chance to speak at the meeting. We all had something exciting to say and we shared our ideas and thoughts of the Hexapod's interior and design. We were shocked to see some of the things we saw. We felt safe on the Hexapod, not just because there were security robots rolling around the place, but because there was an over-abundance of opportunity for us BASIC 12 humans. There were nine guest bathrooms, seven bedrooms, four living room areas, three hall areas, and two huge gyms that could easily hold a battalion of people.

I was scared to touch anything in the guest bathrooms. I just wanted to take pictures with my camera of how grandeur everything looked. The beds on the Hexapod were all king size, and were lavishly constructed. All we could have at home resided on the Hexapod. My homesickness left me once I started using everything on the ship. It was 3000 miles long, 2000 miles wide, and 900 miles in depth. It had so much extra space to satisfy our every need.

So the voyage continued into the space frontier, and the planet Earth was a long way from us, almost out of sight. We were so far into outer space that we were on the ship and did not feel that it was actually moving forward.

* * * *

The BASIC 12 was about to wrap up our meeting and eat together as a whole for the first time on the ship. We had electronic robots in place to serve us. We never had to move from the table, unless we had to excuse ourselves from the room for some reason. We ate healthy foods like baked chicken, orange salmon and baked potatoes. Other foods, like pizza and fried chicken, and soul food recipes were programmed into the robots, as well. We also had healthy food-filling pills that we could take to get full off. All we had to do was command them to serve us. We did not blow a whistle, clap our hands or anything like that. We communicated to them like they were humans. But most of the time they already knew how to respond, because they had micro disks in them that had all the expert housemaid skills programmed into them. If I was going to stay alert on the ship, I could not afford to get lazy. We had too many robots that were like spaceship maids that were on twenty-hour clean-up duty. It was almost like they waited around for something to happen and they'd be there to clean it up, unless the situation was risky, in which case they had common sense data stored in them. This was how sufficient the Hexapod was. The Hexapod made sure we were cared for emotionally, physically, mentally, and spiritually. The Hexa-

Chapter 2

pod even had shower robots in the bathrooms that washed those hard-to-reach spots for us. The robots even had professional masseuse skills better than most human spas and massage parlors. They also played mind games with us, to help us to think better during the voyage.

Anyway, there was nothing said during our meal, since the food was so good.

"The robots did their thing, eh?" Austin uttered.

"Yes, yes, yes!" JL shouted. "These robots are right up there with my granny in cooking skills. My kids would have loved this meal."

We had a different entree at each meal, and then days would go by before the sequence of meals was repeated. So we would get used to something different each day. We did not have to cook or clean either, but we always did, since the robots had automatic sensors that tended to house cleaning duties like housekeepers back in America. Of course, man-made products could fail, so we could not totally rely on the robots to do the job all the time, but they still did while they were in good working order. Most robotic systems slowed down to recharge as soon as every member of the company was asleep. However, other robots recharged during the day and would be on the prowl during the night like night watch security. Some of the robots had visual capabilities like dogs, meaning they could see at a distance at night.

Yet, the robots could not defend themselves and did not have weaponry to fight like humans might. Still, the robots were very helpful in taking care of the little things that made the voyage feel even smoother. It almost seemed like I did not have to worry about a thing, "Why was I even feeling so homesick?" I kept saying to myself.

The BASIC 12 utilized every aspect of the Hexapod, for we found the entertainment features to be over-satisfying. It was like we were at a carnival, but without rides.

Chapter Three:
A Soap Opera in Outer Space

As time passed, we all got well acquainted with our newly made spaceship. We explored the high-class shower rooms and spas, and ate nice meals, as if we were royalty all the time. "Does anybody have this good fortune?" I thought to myself, walking down the large halls of the spaceship. We met every once in a while to discuss the advantages of the spaceship and how effective they were, just to make sure we are all on the same page about things. Even if the Hexapod had its disadvantages, we had no knowledge of such things while on the ship.

We had to perform war rehearsals just in case we had to go to battle. We would zip to our stations just as we were trained at the Warsan Center before launch. The Hexapod had six pods which all did pretty much the same thing. Each was to conduct missile and counterstrike attacks and the release of grenade C4 cannon attacks. In POD 1, which was located in the left north corner of the Hexapod, Paria and Babatunde sat ready and locked in. In POD 2, which was located in the right north corner, Carlos and I sat and we got ready and locked in, as well. In POD 3, which was located in the northwest corner of the ship, JL and Austin also locked into position for battle and got ready to go. In POD 4, which was located in the northeast corner of the spaceship, Hay-Hay and NaHafa sat patiently locked in. In POD 5, which was located on the southeast side of the ship, Yao and A-Rod were comfortably locked, in waiting on a signal

Chapter 3

to fire. The final POD 6, which was on the southwest side of the ship, contained the courageous Manny and Safoya, who would take their time getting locked in. These spots would be named our signature spots throughout the voyage. Each member made his or her own name plates and placed them in the appropriate pod. Every pod had the same equipment.

Therefore, what one member of the company wanted to do from one pod, he or she could also do from any other pod when in an emergency situation. The Hexapod had this advantage primarily for security reasons. All of the pods were equally spaced from each other to keep the ship's balance, and they were all the same size.

We played around with the spaceship's controls, just to make sure that things ran correctly. It was so important that we got to know the spaceship we were on. There were so many buttons to push at each of the six stations, not to mention the main control room, but since we had some training and had learned the blueprint of the spaceship, we already knew how to operate everything effectively. There were buttons to release heat-seeking missile shots and grenade launchers.

Time would elapse during that particular day and we each found something to do to fulfill our leisure desires. There was so much to do in extra-curricular activities on the ship that we could really keep busy and get heavily distracted. JL and I went kickboxing in the gym.

"Are you up for this butt whipping, playa?" I yelled at JL.

"We will just see about that, man!" JL uttered.

And off at it we went, kicking and punching at each other for exercise. We got sweaty and blood crept out of my eyes slowly. "Hey Tevie, maybe we should stop now!" JL said.

"No, no, no, the fun has just begun," I hollered back at JL.

We got through the first round and it seemed like JL was winning. JL fought me like we were enemies or something, like we really hated each other, but we were really friends. I was not looking to win, but to have a good workout. Yet, he really took things out of hand, probably because I had talked all that smack before the fight.

I did not intend to let him win. I just wanted something to do to keep me in great shape on the voyage. He had some good drop kicks, jab combos and uppercuts that had me a little worried.

Times got rough as I took the next four rounds, since he had finally gotten me more interested in the fight and not just the exercise. We had so much fun fighting. It was really a sweat breaker. The whole event was only supposed to go nine rounds, but things got intense. So intense that JL sprang his ankle and I twisted my wrist and busted an eyelid. It was inevitable that the battle stopped there. We both reached for the emergency first-aid kits in the nearby hallway.

"That was one heck of a fight, huh soldier?" JL spoke.

Chapter 3

"It sure was, but we took it out of context," I replied. "Way out of context. We took that fight like there was millions on the line."

"We needed this match reran on KMOP-TV, pay-per-view," JL uttered.

"Yeah, maybe we could've made some dough off that and flipped the money, I responded quickly. For an older man, you really got a nice jab, playa."

"You ain't so bad yourself, young buck," JL said with such pride.

While we were pursuing our kick boxing egos for exercise, Yao and Safoya sat back and ate some of one of Yao's prize winning Chinese food. "I got some good stuff waiting for you to try, you ready, lady?" Yao asked Safoya.

"Yes, I love eating good Chinese food," Safoya said non-hesitantly.

Yao taught Safoya how to properly use chopsticks. They played Chinese Checkers and other games that Safoya made up. "I am so bored, maybe you can show me some of your games and I will show you some of the games that I play back home," Safoya said. Safoya knew of games like Charades and other games.

"This game of Charades, is it like the game of Pictionary, where you use hand motions and clues to solve things?" Yao questioned Safoya.

"You're almost right on it," Safoya answered rapidly. "Yao, how can a gal like me make Chinese food like you, really?"

Yao replied, "Just follow my lead and you will have Chinese food lovers eating out of the palm of your hand, for sure. I would like to learn what a ghetto girl is. I am trying to be more hip, can you show me? Some years ago, when I was younger, my Chinese friends always told me that I was a vegetable or idiot and was not popular enough or hip," Yao explained.

"You are fine just the way you are. Do not let peer pressure drop down the way that you know you want to live," Safoya laughed. "I do not think you want to characterize yourself as that kind of woman. You seem humble to me by appearance. Being hip is not all it is cracked up to be, trust me, I know."

There was no ego issue with Yao, as she was happy when Safoya won at Chinese Checkers. Yao proved to be a fun person to be around because of how friendly she was. They played more and more games and Safoya was not so bored after playing with Yao. Safoya enjoyed eating everything Yao made and enjoyed learning how to make things that Yao cooked for them. They became closer as friends, not just as cadets on a spaceship.

While they were entertaining themselves, NaHafa and A-Rod played rounds of the game Truth or Dare. A-Rod spoke, "Have you ever played this game before?"

NaHafa responded, "I do not know. How do you play it?"

Chapter 3

"Well, we take turns choosing either the Truth or the Dare. Either way you go, it is usually a risky situation, but it is much fun to play amongst people. Okay, let us go at it, this could be interesting," NaHafa said quickly.

A-Rod was the cool but daring type, while NaHafa was shy at times and more about the truth of things. Occasionally she possessed a wild streak that would shock a whole nation, I thought. At least this was how I thought her personality really was.

NaHafa was a nice brown skinned girl, who loved doing daring things. She could be a risk taker and be free at times, yet still seem quiet at the same time. Of course, A-Rod always thought the truth should set you free. This is the kind of mentality that he kept. They asked each other easy questions at first, so that they could be at ease more. Then as the game progressed, the questions and obstacles got tougher for the both of them. Also, the questions got more and more interesting. It got to the point where Nahafa dared A-Rod to kiss her.

A-Rod hesitated, being that he was not sure what NaHafa was after or if something suspicious could start during the voyage. Even though this was just a game, he thought about NaHafa's wishes and respected her as a woman and was not so quickened by lust for her. However, finally, A-Rod and Nahafa kissed, and they fondled each other. NaHafa enjoyed the kiss, even though it was only for the sake of the game that they were playing.

He felt something too. "I cannot believe this game

made us this way," A-Rod whispered to NaHafa.

"Just go with the flow, baby, just go with the flow," NaHafa responded slowly. They softened one another with each other's caress. They held each other as if they did not want anything to come between them. He kissed her neck and then slowly and sensually started taking her clothes off. She commenced to taking off his clothes right there in the corridor of the ship.

Things got more intimate as she licked his spine as if it were ice cream or a lollipop. One thing led to another and it seemed as though a flame had started burning. The flame got more intense as they poured lust onto one another as if they had known each other a long time. They went to a nearby bed just outside the corridor and then their lust continued in a nearby shower room. They got bubbly together in the shower.

Of course, A-Rod was not sure what to think after all that. "I really do not know how to feel right now, lady!" he said to her.

"We are living in the moment, so let us just enjoy it while it lasts okay?" she replied.

"Okay, well, I will scratch your back if you scratch mine!" he answered.

"Okay, let us get something straight, you're going to do more than just scratch my back!" she yelled with confidence.

Chapter 3

Having said that, he just knew he had fun and nothing could stop that. Really, he knew he had a great time. He could not put into words the time he had with her, and how the game made it all occur.

He asked NaHafa how she felt about him. She could not answer, for if she did, she would be cheating herself. Nahafa felt something, but love and a relationship or something further was nonexistent. NaHafa was speechless about it from time to time, and did not want to comment on how good the lovemaking was.

A-Rod was scared to mention anything, too. Nevertheless, he felt a sense of love in NaHafa. But, she was more comfortable about keeping what they had done a secret. NaHafa and A-Rod split away from each other that night quietly, as if nothing had really occurred, but both were shocked about what they had done and how they felt afterward. A-Rod stayed up late, thinking about them in the corridor and in the bathroom and NaHafa had strange dreams about that night. But it did not bother her as much as it bothered A-Rod.

* * * *

Later, A-Rod bumped into Yao and Safoya playing chess in another room. "So y'all are playing chess?" A-Rod spoke.

"We are learning to be better," Safoya and Yao answered. A-Rod joined them in their game, to take his mind off things, but later Yao Ying left because she wanted to do something else. She left Safoya and A-Rod together there.

A-Rod said to Yao, "Why leave so quickly, ma'am?"

Safoya spoke, "Let's play some more."

A-Rod answered, "Yeah, where are you going?"

Yao told them she was getting tired of games. So Safoya and A-Rod were left alone to play more games.

"I guess it is just us two now," A-Rod said.

"It is okay, player. You are up for a game?" Safoya asked.

A-Rod told Safoya that he had played a game of Truth or Dare with NaHafa. She questioned how the game went and he told her it was fine and left it at that.

Safoya asked him, "Who won the game?" He told her it was a stalemate, much like how the chess game was between Safoya and Yao. "Are you sure? There are usually interesting results in that game, for real. I hear about them."

He answered, "Sure, I am sure. Okay, okay, everything was just okay."

"Are you sure you are not hiding something from me?" she asked.

He replied, "Nope and even if I was that is none of your business."

"I guess we should do something else," Safoya continued. "Yeah, let us do that. You seem like you are mad."

"No way," A-Rod said.

Chapter 3

Safoya was tired of the board games and wanted to play an athletic sport. She liked the game of tennis, so she asked A-Rod if he could play tennis and he told her he did not know how. She got all of the equipment ready to play from the various locker rooms in the corridors along the main floor. She figured he did not know how to play, so she was willing to teach him.

They went to the indoor tennis court in the gymnasium to play. He gave her a hard time at first about the whole thing, because he was getting tired and he knew about the long day he had. She teased him and got him all bothered, and he really wanted to play. Something about Safoya knew how to mess with any man's ego, to get him to do something. Just like men can find ways to charm a lady, Safoya knew how to push the buttons on a man to get him to do her bidding.

They set up the tennis net together and were about to play. She gave A-Rod the racket and let him take some swings at tennis balls. A-Rod swung strangely, so she attempted to stand behind him and steer his stroke with the racket. Of course, he failed miserably at tennis so she would get the automatic machine out.

"Okay, if you're ever going to learn this game, you must hit the tennis ball like you do not like it," Safoya said.

"I am doing the best I can madam," A-Rod responded quickly.

She got behind A-Rod and reached around his waist.

"I think I like these lessons you're giving me," A-Rod spoke.

She guided his wrist to swing the ball correctly. Of course, A-Rod loved this even more, because she was buckled around his body so tight. He did not know whether she was trying to teach him or make a pass at him and he was confused. He made her show him more and more and more and he loved the feel of her body around his. She felt good and soft and smelled great.

A-Rod got into a rhythm and started to learn the game better. "I think I am getting better at playing tennis," he said. "What do you think?"

"You are not on my level, but I can see some improvement," she said to him.

"You are no Arthur Ashe, lady. I have seen professionals play way better than you!" he replied. She contested his capabilities by playing him a game or two and he won both games.

"I guess you are getting better than I thought," Safoya spoke. "You get ready to play some more now," she said to him with confidence. She wanted to play again, but he said, "No thanks." She drew stakes with him by making an interesting bet that made it hard for A-Rod to refuse.

Of course, A-Rod would ask her what she was suggesting. "Hey now, what are you up to?" A-Rod said curiously.

Chapter 3

She gave him an option. She said that, if she won, he would have to do anything she said. And if A-Rod won, she would have to do anything he asked. This was the agreement Safoya suggested, but A-Rod was not interested in accepting her proposal for a few reasons. However, he took the deal, anyway.

They played a full tennis game again, and this time Safoya took no prisoners. "Why are you playing me so hard!" A-Rod yelled. "You are playing me now, like you hate me and one million dollars is up for whoever wins this."

"Well, the skills I taught you got me playing hard and for real, and plus there is a deal on the line that I want to win," Safoya explained. She took the first set and he took the next two, winning 6-4 and 6-3. She won the next two, scoring 6-4 in both sets, and A-Rod was sweaty, filthy and tired.

"Well, I see you cannot take the heat this flame is throwing, huh?" Safoya said boastfully.

"I guess you win the bet, because I am bushed," A-Rod said slowly. Therefore, A-Rod listened to Safoya's request. "Okay, what do you want me to do, I am all yours?"

She ordered him to follow her up to the shower room, and he did so. It was almost like she had him on a leash at this point and she was running the show. When they both made it to the shower room, she ordered him to take off her clothes slowly and touch her softly.

"Hey, if this is punishment, I would hate to see what

is not!" he said happily.

"Shut up and keep doing as I ask of you," Safoya said.

"Yes madam, yes madam," A-Rod responded quickly.

Once they were both undressed, they got in the tub. Then, she ordered him to rub her back with lotion and he did so, nice and smoothly. She stood naked before him and he was overwhelmed by her nice shape. He did not think of her in a sexual way at first, but then the torch was lit. He started licking her neck and rubbing her softly, as if she was mink. Her skin was smooth and the lotion made her feel like she was floating in outer space.

"Does all of this feel good to you, Safoya?" A-Rod said.

"It feels like I am in heaven already; do not stop!" Safoya responded.

He rubbed her neck and worked his way down to her shoulders. She had a lean-athletic upper physique that A-Rod admired. He constantly rubbed in the same spot, teasing her, and she told him to go lower and lower. He got to her buttocks and she flipped over. She ordered him to touch her breasts, and so he did, touching them as though to protect them from breaking.

He seduced her and his mouth went everywhere on her body. It seemed like he would suck her dry to fulfill her

Chapter 3

pleasures, if need be. She seduced him the same way and showed him that the whole tennis match was foreplay to get him.

"You knew that game was only a game to get you in this tub with me, right?" Safoya said.

"Sure, and I was so tired and I'm still tired but loving this right now," A-Rod explained.

She really wanted to get him in bed. They continued to make passionate love and more feelings arose. They moved the lovemaking to the bedroom and it got more intense. It was like fireworks and cannons after that. They finished in each other's arms, holding onto the moment as if it were their last breaths. They asked each other what they thought about having a relationship. A-Rod loved how Safoya acted out the whole thing to get with him and he started to have more feelings toward Safoya.

A-Rod was trying to forget the incident earlier that evening with NaHafa, but his mind would not let him forget about her. But he did not tell Safoya about it, since he thought it might damage any future they might have. He had to keep it a secret now or else. Now, he was more confused than ever. Should he stick it out with NaHafa or keep making passionate love with Safoya? "I am really stuck in a bind," A-Rod thought to himself.

Safoya would've liked to start something with A-Rod, but somehow she wasn't really sure if he wanted the same thing. "Do you think we can have some sort of relationship together, A-Rod?" Safoya questioned.

"I am not sure at this point," A-Rod answered quickly. She sensed that he would not love her the way she wanted to be loved. Nevertheless, A-Rod came to her later and agreed to start a relationship with her, because she seemed more like someone he would like to date. She was good looking and smart and knew how to treat a man like a man.

A-Rod left Safoya's quarters and went back to his own quarters. Safoya tossed and turned in her bed, not knowing that A-Rod was gone. Furthermore, guess who was waiting at his door with her blanket?

"NaHafa, what are you doing at my door, lady?" A-Rod said quietly.

She told A-Rod that she couldn't sleep and that she could never really sleep well since their night together. She said that, when she made love, she liked to wake up next to a man.

"Whenever you made love to a man, you always woke up with the man lying next to you?" A-Rod asked.

"Yes always, that is how I like it to be," NaHafa explained.

A-Rod felt bad because he did not know whom to call his mate.

"Is there something wrong, A-Rod?" NaHafa asked.

"No, why do you ask?" A-Rod said.

"You seem a little down and tired, if I might be so

Chapter 3

bold to say," NaHafa said truthfully.

He kept his emotions for Safoya and NaHafa locked in his heart and mind, knowing it was difficult and complicated to be in love with two women at the same time. He just wished it was possible to be in love with two people forever, but it was not. Nevertheless, A-Rod picked NaHafa up in his arms like Superman and carried her to his bed. They went to sleep together until the next morning.

"Now that is how two people in love should wake up," NaHafa noted. "You see how this feels, me lying next to you like this?"

"I know, this does feel nice, but where is breakfast?"

"Y'all men are unbelievable," NaHafa said.

"What made you say that?" A-Rod questioned.

"Food, sex and watching sports is what y'all are all about, right?" NaHafa spoke.

"No, not really. I just happen to be hungry and it's morning," A-Rod said. "I love a good breakfast to get the day going."

They made love again and this time was better than last time for both of them. A-Rod did not know for whom to have emotions, since he now loved two people.

* * * *

Meanwhile, I tried to forget about the pain in my eyelid and my wrist, and workout some more. Safoya saw me and questioned me about working out so late. "Why do you come and lift weights so late?" Safoya mentioned to me.

"Well, I am a workaholic, if there is such a word," I explained. "No really, I like my cuts and do not like to be lean or fat, so this is why I hit the weights and workout so much." I told her I liked my shape and not just for the dime pieces, either. I liked being physically fit for anything I had to face. I refused to be slow and sluggish some billion miles away from Earth.

Safoya was eager to feel my biceps and all the muscular parts of my body. "Man, you are solid as a rock!" Safoya appreciated my physique. I tried to avoid her, but she stripped naked right in front of me and I was weak. I gave in to her body.

"So you look like that under them clothes?" I said shocked. She had a figure any man would want to be next to.

We ran away to another place in the Hexapod to make out slowly, softly and tenderly. I was eager to take my time with her, because I was still having bad dreams and thoughts that something really bad might happen while I was on the ship. Even though I was married, I still felt I had a chance with Safoya, so I took it. She had better curves and a better body than my wife. I kept saying to myself, "I am married."

Nevertheless, I knew I would not see my wife for a while, so I gave in to the ordeal. I was trying to survive and be pleasured at the same time. I knew it was a bad thing to

Chapter 3

do and I would pay for it later. I felt so confused and lost about many things, not just cheating on my wife. But Safoya thought that the way I made love would be good, so that is why she took that risk. Once she saw how muscular I was, she thought about all that energy in the bedroom. But she soon realized she did not like me being rough with her and she asked me to leave. It was hard for her to get me to leave at first, because I wanted to finish what she had started.

"Hey Tevie, this was a mistake," Safoya screamed.

"You made your own mistake," I added. "You set up this moment for us to be intimate, remember?"

"I know, I know, but it is so wrong to do this," Safoya responded. She loved how softly and gingerly A-Rod touched her, and how A-Rod listened to her orders. She remembered that and it stuck to her like glue. She liked how she had controlled the situation when she was with A-Rod. But when she made love to me, it seemed like I controlled the whole thing and this bothered her.

Later that night, Safoya cried alone in her quarters, thinking about the lustful moves that she had made with me. "What is wrong with me? What am I turning into?" Safoya said calmly to herself in fear.

Nevertheless, NaHafa woke up in A-Rod's arms and they kissed and hugged each other gently. NaHafa left and went to take a shower in her quarters after telling A-Rod that she loved him.

A-Rod thought, "How could one fall in love with

someone else so quickly? This could not be! Or could it?" he thought. He felt like he could possibly love her, but he was not ready for all that, at least not yet. In his mind, he was in love with no one. "Love can be like cancer or AIDS, it can break you down and kill you," he thought to himself. "I really do not know what to think or how to feel," he said to himself.

He questioned the number of sexual encounters he'd had and why. He was trying to figure out how he could get out of the lustful triangle he was caught in, but it was difficult to take all of it in. His personality and rhythm was distorted because of it all. He knew he had dug himself deeper and the soap opera type situation was literally playing with his emotions and his mind. He knew he was in the midst of a scandal in outer space. It was like an old school episode of the daytime soap opera, Passions.

* * * *

JL, Paria, and Austin were playing Spades and Backgammon in one of the other entertainment areas. JL won most of the games, yet Paria might still win a few.

"Well, Paria, are you tired of losing yet?" JL said with confidence.

"Almost, deal me some good hands and I will surely make some interesting games come about quickly.

"We cannot play all these different types of card games!" Austin uttered. "I am too sure that this ship has everything that we need and want, so I am sure it has more

Chapter 3

games to play," he added.

"Yep, there are!" Paria replied. "But we are just not playing those games at the moment!"

"Can we do something else?" Austin spoke out. "I am tired of the card game extravaganza."

"Soon!" JL answered quickly. "We are really into these games right now, or at least I am."

"Okay, I am cutting out at this point!" Austin yelled. "Do what you will, bro!"

"We still got more games to go!" JL said.

So Austin left JL and Paria to play more card games and went to the super sauna rooms that were located near the rear of the hexapod's second floor.

* * * *

In another part of the ship, Yao was having a long night's rest, away from all the drama that A-Rod and Safoya were going through. Yao stayed to herself a lot and paid more attention to the mission. She did not want to get distracted by anything or any drama. She literally dodged it all.

Now, I had broken my vow to my wife a second time, but it didn't matter to me anymore. I kept saying to myself, "What have I done?" Even more than that, Safoya did not like the way I loved her. It seemed bad to her. It was looking like I had wasted my time, cheating for nothing, and I ended up getting cheated, it seemed.

I was already a mess, because I never felt right on the voyage anyway. I always felt that something bad was still going to happen. As for Ms. Safoya Sarayova, she was so wrapped up in her sexual encounters with some of the people on the ship that she eventually seduced Manny, as well. She saw Manny in the hall, and she was feeling down about the situation with A-Rod and me. She started crying and Manny fondled her and hugged her close, so intimately that they began to kiss.

"Why are we doing this?" Manny said while kissing her.

"I do not know," Safoya replied. "Because it feels right, right now maybe!"

"We should not be doing this," Manny spoke. "I do feel something a little different right now!"

"So you know what I mean?" Safoya continued.

"Yes, I guess," Manny replied. The encounter with Manny came as no surprise, as Manny was eager to see how good she was in the bedroom department. "You know I have dreamed about when this day might happen, but never thought I would have the chance," Manny said.

"Well now, sweetheart, you got your chance. So what will you do about it?" Safoya answered.

He picked her up in his arms gently and they proceeded to another hallway on the next floor, away from everyone

Chapter 3

else. "Is this a good spot to finish what we started?" Manny added.

"Yes, I guess," Safoya responded.

"And she was great, without a doubt," he said to me later. "She really stands up to her figure," he added when he saw me. This move put her at risk to be somewhat of a slut on the Hexapod.

Meanwhile, I was lifting weights in the gymnasium, hoping I would forget the encounter I'd had with Safoya. But the more I tried to forget about it the more it haunted me. I had daydreams and nightmares about it, too. How could she keep all those secrets to herself and not feel anything, not care about her self-respect? She must be a Virgo to keep so many secrets, I thought to myself.

* * * *

Babatunde Alfa and Carlos Lopez were sound asleep in their quarters. Resting faithfully, like they were true, innocent brothers that never made any trouble at all. BA loved to sleep long hours, especially if he felt he was too tired to move. Carlos was just too tired and felt like he needed a nap.

Later, BA and Carlos met up in the game room. "Are you down for some matches of Ping Pong?" Carlos questioned.

"I am not that good at this game!" BA replied. "You need to bring that energy to the basketball court. Now that is a real man's game."

"You ready to lose right now at Ping Pong or what?" Carlos asked.

"Let us go at it. Bring it on!" BA said with confidence. And BA beat Carlos Lopez at Ping Pong 3 to 2. "Now I have beaten you at your own game. How does it feel?" BA questioned.

"That is okay, now how about them hoops?" Carlos answered. To try making up for his losses, Carlos played basketball and seemed pretty good at first. Yet, he could not beat BA. BA had all-around game. "Hey, I can play a little ball, but I see I am not as good as you," Carlos said to BA.

"You really did shock me here in the gym," BA answered. "You played better than I thought you would play, so that is a plus from me to you."

"Maybe some other time you can let me win, huh?" Carlos said.

"Not a chance. I never just let people I play win at this game," BA added quickly.

After their basketball fiasco, they retreated to the showers and then returned to their quarters. Eventually, BA and Carlos got back in bed to rest. It seemed that they slept as if they had a whole day ahead of them.

* * * *

Hay-Hay was awake, playing electronic video games

Chapter 3

to his heart's content. Hay-Hay was a true video game addict. He was a curious, detective type person. He loved fighting and adventure games. He was the type who would throw the controller, if his performance was not well while playing. He liked the investigative games because they were the most interesting.

"You are sure into those video games, cadet!" Yao said when she spotted Hay-Hay in the game room.

"Call it whatever you will, I love this stuff and that is real," Hay-Hay replied quickly.

One night Hay-Hay spied on Safoya like a detective on a big drug bust, and he saw her sneak into A-Rod's room. When Hay-Hay saw this he was in awe. He sat there like a hawk or a seeing eye-dog. Staring hard, he watched her come to my room also. "Huh, I wonder what is all that about? Why is Safoya going from quarter to quarter in the middle of the night, to married mens' rooms?" Hay-Hay asked himself.

It seemed funny that Safoya was that much of a slut, tossing her body around the way she was. "It just does not make sense to me," Hay-Hay said to himself, shocked. But he was a shrewd fellow, as well, he wanted in on the action, so he blackmailed Safoya. He left his quarters and cut her off sneaking around.

"What are you doing jumping quarters like this?" Hay-Hay questioned Safoya.

"Um, I don't know," Safoya said in amazement.

He replied, "I already know what you are up to and it is no good, for real. If you're going to all of the male quarters, why not come to mine and drop me off a sample or something? I saw you in those nice night clothes, coming out of two male quarters."

Safoya realized that Hay-Hay knew what she was up to, so she listened to all of his demands. Hay-Hay promised to keep it all hush-hush.

She pleased him, too, giving him whenever and whatever he wanted, and thinking nothing of his wife and kids.

Hay-Hay proved to be a sneaky rat and before this Safoya did not think Hay-Hay could be that sneaky and ferocious, blackmailing her and disrespecting his family at the same time. "Why do you choose to be dirty like me?" Safoya asked Hay-Hay.

"This is actually fun to me," Hay-Hay added. "I really got a taste of what I had been wanting to try for a long time, you."

"What is your problem? What about your wife?" Safoya added.

"That lady is I don't know how many miles away right now, and you seem like the next best thing. Tell me something, if you were in my situation, how you would have handled it?"

Safoya answered, "But don't you care about my respect."

"It seems like you've made some married men lose respect for you and their wives, as well," Hay-Hay spoke. "So where does that leave your respect for their wives and yourself? I think your respect is in the dumps, if you ask me."

"Now you are just as dirty as me and I do not need any fans of such bad things," Safoya added.

"Well, at least I am not confused about who I am in love with."

Safoya knew she had things messed up now. She'd had a taste of nearly every male on the ship. She felt as filthy as dirty rags. Nevertheless, she was truly pleased with the way Hay-Hay made love to her and wanted to go at it again. But Hay-Hay was not in love with her. He had just wanted a sample. He'd only lusted after her because he knew he could get away with it and have fun at the same time.

"You are such a dog to me now," Safoya told Hay-Hay.

"RUFF, RUFF, GRRRR!" Hay-Hay yelled, teasing Safoya. "Call me whatever you want, but the joke is still on you. I don't have a bad heart about any of this and you still want to be with me right now, don't you?" Hay-Hay questioned.

"Yes, I am so sad to say." Safoya replied, surrendering.

"But I cannot do this. I am not really a dirty man, but I

played the game and it seems I still came out a winner. Even though you now think I am a loser," Hay-Hay explained. "But the buck stops here, and I will keep this a secret for as long as I can bear."

* * * *

Another Hexapod attack drill sounded soon after that and everybody took to their battle stations.

"Battle alarm! Everyone to your stations quickly!" Captain Paria Ponga shouted loudly.

Safoya and Hay-Hay ended their conversation and went to their own pods. It was really just a drill to see how fast people could get to their stations.

"Is everybody locked in?" Paria shouted.

Everyone responded, "We are locked in, captain, and we are ready to hear your commands."

"We need to try to be faster each time," Paria added. "It is important that we do this thing effectively and efficiently, with no hassle or struggle. Remember that our lives are at stake and if everything is not done correctly, bad things could happen."

While Paria talked to us over the intercom, I thought about the fact that I still had a slight limp when I walked, because my ankle was still in pain. Since the robots on the ship were trained in physical therapy, I caught a robot and ordered it to come to me. The robot started by giving me a foot message. Next, it twisted my ankle to the left and the right, until

Chapter 3

it popped. "Wow, that feels good. Right there, right there!" The robot rubbed and pressed its hands onto my ankle and worked for hours. My ankle got better and stronger. I could tell that the swelling was receding and my leg was healing. I started taking fewer pills and my eye was getting better, also. I felt like my strength was coming back.

Shortly after that, Paria called us to eat together at the table, while we had a BASIC 12 meeting. We were all talking around the table.

"Order! Attention everybody!" Paria yelled. All was quiet and Paria began speaking. "I would like to thank everybody for making the trip a success, so far. I just want to say, I hope everybody is having some kind of fun on this ship. This ship seems too big for us and you can really stretch out and relax here."

Of course, she did not know about the lustful trials taking place between A-Rod and Safoya, A-Rod and Nahafa, Safoya and Manny, Safoya and Hay-Hay, and Safoya and me. She was sure that emotions would not get out of hand during supper because she assumed that everybody was having a good time.

Everybody went back to talking to one other around the table. Safoya looked at Hay-Hay and he looked back at her with a sneaky eye, as if he was up to something. He looked at her and then he looked at Paria.

However, Hay-Hay caused the commotion that let the cat out of the bag, because no one else really knew that Safoya had slept with so many men. Hay-Hay said, "There is a slut on the ship that has turned this voyage into a daytime soap and this is not 'As the World Turns.' There is some game playing on this ship and it is not baseball." He did not say anyone's name.

Paria was shocked by what she heard and she started questioning the table like she was Judge Judy.

A-Rod spoke first by saying that he was sorry about all he had done. "I feel so uneasy right now."

"What did you do?" Paria asked. "I do not understand what you are saying."

He felt so pitiful saying it, but he knew the truth hurt. All the encounters he'd had with Safoya and Nahafa were burning him up inside, like a hot air balloon about to burst. "I cannot take this anymore!" A-Rod said. "I am mentally breaking down fast and I cannot take it!" He told Paria that he'd had sex with both Safoya and NaHafa, but that he had no feelings for Safoya. It was only an issue of lust with Safoya.

I could see the weakness in A-Rod's emotions and Safoya could too. She took it all in with pride, even if A-Rod considered NaHafa to be his woman now.

"I realize that I have feelings for NaHafa only," A-Rod. At first, he was not sure with whom to be with, but now he knew for sure.

I was blasted by the news and as I tried to storm out of the room Paria quickly ordered me to sit back down. I felt

Chapter 3

badly because I was secretly wrapped up in the same kind of drama. I felt shameful for cheating on my wife and I felt even more shameful that the lady I'd cheated with did not have true feelings for me. She was angry with me because I'd called her a slut, but when women sleep with many men, there are certain words used to describe them. I prayed to God for understanding. I knew I had done wrong and I wanted some guidance and direction. It seemed like I actually felt worse than A-Rod.

Really, at this point, the whole ship needed praying for, including me. We were beside ourselves and the mission was starting to smell like spoiled meat.

Later, after the meeting, I approached Safoya in the hallway. "Why toss your body around like that?"

Hay-Hay overheard us talking and ran over to us, saying, "Do not worry, I had a little piece of the action, too!"

"What?" I shouted. "Him, too?"

"Unfortunately, he is telling the truth," Safoya said sadly.

"Oh my gosh!" I said like a madman. "Well Safoya, who can you really love? You have done half of the ship." I was so angry that I was scared of what I might do next. I wished I had not had sex with her, for now I feel so much shame it was almost unbearable. I had allowed temptation to get in my way. I still felt uneasy and it was getting worse. I was thinking to myself, what is the worse that can happen now? To think, I'd had sex with a lady who'd had sex with more than three people and that made me feel immoral.

Paria called everyone back to the meeting and had everyone formally apologize to the table, reminding us that we still had to work as a team. "It does not matter who sleeps with whom, we still must finish this voyage," Paria said. "We must stick it out together as a team on this mission. We should all agree that what happens on the ship ought to stay on the ship, and that is that."

A-Rod told everyone that his true girlfriend was NaHafa and NaHafa saw the sincerity in his emotions as he said it. Safoya was left alone to think about what she had done, because she knew I was angry with her, as were many others she had been with on the ship. Hay-Hay and Manny never really had feelings for her. She was just a one-night stand to each of them, really. Now the whole soap opera was out in the open and Safoya was glad because she was tired of sneaking around.

Yao was still shocked that Safoya would throw her body around the way she had. "How are you feeling there, lady?" Yao said with care.

"I am feeling better, I guess," Safoya answered with grief.

Yao had developed tremendous feelings for her, but hearing the news had caused her feelings to fade.

At this point, Safoya was extremely angry with Hay-Hay. She had known the whole fiasco wouldn't stay a secret forever. "I feel like a different person than when I first set

Chapter 3

foot on this ship," she said to herself in a room. She hadn't known she was capable of seducing so many men in just a matter of hours.

Paria caught up with Safoya and told her, "Stop throwing your body around and stay with one person and one person only. It is not healthy being a working girl for every man. I have been down that road before and I know where it leads, and it is never a pretty ending. I have been a waitress in a bar and a flight attendant in my past. I am now an old hen," she said. "I was once attracted to this guy that I thought would be my king. He gave me money and great love, but he had nothing else to give worth keeping in my heart. It broke my heart to see him make out with another girl right in front of me," she added. "But it does not really matter because he did not give me anything I could hold in my heart. So it wasn't like he was cheating on me, really." She was trying to tell Safoya about what it meant to be heartbroken and cheated on, because she hated when people slept around. Somehow Paria forgave Safoya, but she still told her to cool it.

* * * *

The soap opera had been exposed and now A-Rod felt more relieved than he had felt in days. He felt like Safoya had gotten the best of him and made him weak, even though he was in control of the situation.

JL was heart-stricken by the men who'd had sex outside of their marriage. "I am so shocked by what went down by some of our company members," JL said. "As if we do not have enough fun things to do on this ship already. I guess some of the husbands on this ship could not wait to get back to their lawfully wedded wives, so they made Safoya a victim of lust. I still cannot figure out why they treated her like that."

We knew we were in the wrong. JL looked at Hay-Hay, Manny and with no respect, like there was no way we could fix what we had done.

Chapter Four:
The Untouchable's Intro

All was calm on our Hexapod. It was so quiet you could hear the echoes of our breath while we were eating in the large conference room. After dinner, Hay-Hay and Safoya attacked one another in the gym, as to show their anger against one another. Safoya would not let Hay-Hay forget how angry she was, but neither would be severely hurt.

"See, I have to teach you a lesson or two about blackmailing a fair lady," Safoya said with revenge in her heart.

"So what are you going to do about it?" Hay-Hay challenged. "Ouch," he yelled a second later. "Why punch me so hard?"

"Now you know what my feelings are towards you," she explained.

"Okay, I see," Hayward replied.

Wam! Wam! Wack! Safoya landed punches on Hay-Hay, he fell and his face was cut and bruised. "Next time you will think before you blackmail the wrong sister. Now I feel so much better about what you did to me."

JL burst into the gym and broke them up quickly, and then had them make up.

"I did not know you had such power in kickboxing," Hay-Hay told Safoya.

But just as Safoya was about to punch Hay-Hay once

Chapter 4

more, JL told them, "Remember what Paria said, we are all in this together."

Safoya called Hay-Hay "a hater" and he called her a daytime soap opera slut. Then he apologized when JL ordered him to. This sort of scenario continued between them for a while but as time passed, they became used to being around one another.

* * * *

After a while, Paria spotted something on the radar. "Hey company, I think we've caught a glitch."

Carlos and JL spotted it, too. "Wow! What is that?" some of the company replied.

"It looks like a UFO," JL added. "We are not ready for a UFO."

The spacecraft was big enough to outweigh the Hexapod and it seemed more powerful. "The spaceship seems highly developed," Yao said. "I tried to investigate the history of the UFO, with no luck. Anything we learn about this UFO will be classified information. I do not know if anyone has files about this UFO."

"So you mean to tell me that we got something coming right at us that we know nothing about?" Austin uttered.

"I am afraid so, Austin," Paria replied. "Our ship can handle this thing, can't it Yao?"

"I am not sure, company. Our sensor protectors aren't

giving the right responses," Yao said. Although the Hexapod had many more advantages, this particular UFO had powers that could breech the Hexapod.

"Where did it go?" Safoya responded as it disappeared into outer space.

"It looks pretty fast and snappy," Paria yelled. It could fly in hyperspace ten times faster than our Hexapod.

"Okay y'all, we are up against something, for real," JL explained. "We've got no time to think about the soap opera drama, so forget about it now."

We saw the UFO coming at us fast and we did not have time to create a force field to protect us from attack.

"Why can't we get this UFO on radar?" Austin added. "I thought we were number one in technological advances? Y'all are talking like the ship is plotting to destroy us. What to do now, Paria?"

"I am not sure at this point, since its actions are not drastic."

Our advantages did not mean a thing compared to the enormous power of this ship. I sat there with the rest of the team, looking at how swiftly the UFO vanished. Nevertheless, we got our targets ready to fire if need be.

"I am so uneasy about this one," Paria mumbled.

"We will keep a close watch on this thing and see how it reacts," Hay-Hay murmured.

Chapter 4

"Do not take your eyes off of it for one minute, and record just about everything different that you see," Paria ordered Hay-Hay. The UFO was still a great distance away. But we noticed that it was getting closer as time passed, since it was getting bigger and bigger on our screen. "Hay-Hay, record all the changes thus far, because things have changed."

"That UFO is getting closer?" he yelled. "Holy mackerel! Let us ring the alarm quickly!"

All of the Basic 12 were fully aware of the UFO in pursuit and were ready for anything to happen. We were hoping our defense was just as effective as we believed they would be.

Paria told everybody, "We are all in this together, through thick and thin." The rest of us responded with a resounding yes. Paria continued, "Put all of your energy into what is coming up ahead and not what has happened in the past. This UFO is one thing, but whatever is inside the UFO is another thing to understand."

"Paria is right, that ship is not moving on its own," JL added. "Whatever is in that ship, its got some brains, for sure. We are not messing with a dummy here, please believe! We must be careful about whatever this is we are dealing with."

Using my supervision space binoculars, I was able to see that, residing inside the huge UFO, there was a six-foot, nine-inch solid alien-like monster with human-like features. "Hey y'all, it looks like there's a human in that ship!" I explained. "Hey wait a minute, it seems half human, half alien. Someone else may need to get a look at this to make sure I am not going crazy."

"Hey cadet, gimme those binoculars!" Carlos uttered. "Wow, Tevie is not playing about this one, I think everybody should look at this. I wish I could take some pictures, but it is so far away."

"Okay, now that y'all have seen the monster, what's next?" Austin added. "I know we are here for exploration and seeking new ideas and technology, but what we are seeing and experiencing now baffles me."

"Hey there, kiddo, it's all good. Everything will be alright, so do not worry your little head off," JL said.

To me, the monster looked strong. Its head was big and shaped like a human's, and its whole body was covered in sharp, stringy tentacles thin enough to slice a sheet of paper. It seemed determined to get to its destination, moving faster than the speed of light. My sight could not catch up with its movements. I relayed all of this to the company as it guided its triangular-shaped UFO closer to our Hexapod.

"Hey y'all, it seems that it is getting closer and closer!" Austin alerted.

The ship had special features that could actually surprise the Hexapod at any time, missiles and heat-seekers that could come from the rear of the ship. The location of the missiles and heat-seekers was unknown, but we had our focus on its frontal view. We had no clue that it had weapons

Chapter 4

and defensive mechanisms that were better and more powerful than our Hexapod.

It shot a beam that was twenty-two miles long in length from a distance of two hundred thirty billion kilometers. We were able to see that its right wing was more powerful than its left wing, since its left wing was for poisoning and egg-placing for its defeated subjects. The alien was female, since it had eggs and a female sense of reproduction, but strangely, it had no gender. It could create offspring from a cell-structured source.

It wasn't capable of using common sense, though. It had never seen a human being before and it did not know how to treat one or how to handle itself. It didn't know what humans looked like, how humans were supposed to smell or why humans existed.

We hoped to find something extraordinary on the voyage, but we never really thought we would come across something so extraterrestrial as this. I had the feeling that things were going to be changing drastically, but I did not know when and I was uneasy about the present situation. Now I knew why I had always felt that something bad was going to happen.

While in the Hexapod, we ate with one eye on our meal and kept the other on the UFO.

"Hey, it seems like that creature has calmed down for a while," Austin noted.

"I am not sure of that, and I am not resting on that,"

JL answered Austin. Yet, JL asked the company, "Who is behind the stirring wheel of that big ship? I mean, what is that ugly thing we saw through those binoculars?" he shouted with fear.

I could not give him an answer but I had seen something that was hard to describe. We all had, and we certainly had no words for it. We sat there in awe thinking about it and how dangerous it might be. The size of the UFO made the Hexapod look as if it should not have existed, it was really that big.

"That is a mighty big UFO!" I told the rest of the company. Even though the alien had two human-like arms, its tentacles could reach across a city or town, if need be. They were long and slimy, and there was a liquid substance leaking from its monstrous body. It looked gruesome to the human eye. The alien monster, to me, was known as The Untouchable.

* * * *

Meanwhile, somewhere else in the Hexapod several of the company were getting ready for bed and others shifted to the entertainment center of the ship.

"Some will sleep and some will watch," Paria said. "JL and Carlos will dictate the duties of who will watch and who will sleep and rotate." I could tell that Paria was getting more serious about this creature and wanted the best alert possible to make sure that everybody was cared for and accounted for. "We need to know if that ship or that thing inside that ship moves," Paria added. "We should have

Chapter 4

more than one person watching. Forget about guarding any security check points around our spaceship." She wanted to make sure that all the astronauts were well rested, so they'd be alert when in battle.

There were automatic security cameras all around the Hexapod, so that we could keep close tabs on the UFO. Of course, A-Rod was excited about all that had happened so far and was anxious to be part of every command Paria gave him. "So when do we battle this weird-looking UFO?" A-Rod said to Paria.

"I do not know," Paria replied nervously.

His worries about the past soap opera-like events had long gone astray. He looked at the current matter as the bigger issue now. "This is way more interesting than that crap I went through with Safoya! I am ready to go at this creature so bring it on! I do not care how big and tall it is, it is like Goliath and I am like David. Besides, whatever that thing is, it must have a weakness, and we must find out what it is quickly." A-Rod wanted the ship to draw nearer so we could all see the UFO and the so-called Untouchable up close, with our very own eyes.

With half of us resting, Safoya talked to Yao about the exact size of the UFO, but she could not give a definite answer. Yao responded, "The coordinates of the location of the ship is a little off, but we are still in the direction of that UFO, for sure." She still could not give the size of the thing. "Our sensors are not picking it up too well."

"You mean to tell me that this creature has jamming

techniques, too?" JL exclaimed. "That means we are going to lose much sleep on this thing, for sure!" The monster itself seemed hard to measure since its tentacles seemed like a force field for its whole body. They could not get the coordinates of where the monster was inside the ship, either.

"So he really could be plotting on us and we do not know its whereabouts?" Austin questioned.

"I am afraid so, cadet. I am afraid so," Yao answered.

Austin asked, "Where did something like that come from, and why is it headed this way?"

Paria replied, "I have no answer for that, I only wish to find answers to that and more."

Hay-Hay radioed Paria to ask, "When will the battle take place?"

Paria could not give a designated time of battle, which JL and Carlos thought was odd, because it looked like the UFO was getting extremely close and ready to attack.

"It is getting closer and closer," Hay-Hay yelled.

"We cannot jump to conclusions," she continued, "it has not made any attempts to attack us, so why try to destroy it first?"

Hay-Hay responded, "Maybe we should do something before it is too late." We were all in a state of fear because we were unsure of what the thing might do next.

Chapter 4

Carlos shouted, "Everybody return to his or her position," and everyone did so immediately. "Do not get distracted and stay in communication by television or visa-screen, so we can locate each other's positions. Be careful about this situation and at the same time pay attention to it." We did not know what to expect from this UFO or what was inside of it. "Keep your eyes and ears peeled for any suspicious activity."

"I guess I should say thanks to Carlos for stepping in," Paria added calmly over the intercom. "If anyone has opinions or ideas, they should bring them to the discussion over the intercom, because they may be crucial in events like this. If there is anytime to be serious about something, this is it. Be serious about what is up ahead! I know I should be more sincere about this whole thing, and I apologize for that. We need to act quickly, because we do not know what that ship or that thing inside of it is capable of."

Our visual sensors couldn't see inside the alien's ship like my binoculars had earlier, but I'd lost them somewhere on the ship and I could not find them. The monster had become smarter and it had put up black barriers to block our visual sensors from looking inside its ship. So none of us could see inside the ship anymore, binoculars or not.

We ate all of our meals in each of our prospective pods, so we could watch the approaching UFO draw nearer rather quickly. Austin stated, "I never knew a ship could move so fast. So much for trying to make an escape from this ship, if we had to."

Indeed, time went by and some of the BASIC 12 got sleepy again. "Aye, we need some Z's," Safoya and NaHafa uttered.

"Yep, I think we need to make it off to dreamland, as well," A-Rod and I replied.

"Besides, if some of us do not get the required sleep, how will we have the energy needed to go up against this estranged UFO?" A-Rod added.

"I hear you," Paria replied.

Safoya and I rushed to our quarters, and NaHafa and A-Rod rushed into his quarters. The thirty-minute quickie they had was both to see if their love for each other was still meant to be and just in case it was the last time they could make love.

"It seems like we are rushing this moment," A-Rod said.

"Just kiss me over and over," NaHafa said passionately.

"Whatever you say, ma'am!" A-Rod said boldly.

"I am glad we went through that soap opera fiasco," NaHafa mentioned.

"What do you mean?" A-Rod shouted while lying in bed with her.

"Now I know who my true love is and why," she added, "I know who I can have feelings for and show them."

Chapter 4

"Shouldn't you be more worried about this monster lurking around our ship?"

"I am worried about that too, but I still love you," NaHafa noted smoothly.

"Stop making me feel soft and guilty at the same time" he added.

They ran off to an enclosed area of the ship, where A-Rod snatched off NaHafa's spaceship wear and undergarments, and she fondled and caressed his body.

"Hey dear, you are so aggressive, you must want me badly," NaHafa said.

"It is all this emotion you've filled me up with that's got me acting this way," A-Rod said. "I do not know where it came from, but I love it. We cannot do this for too long, for we really should get some rest soon."

"I know we will have to report back shortly, but we are seizing the great moments we have together," NaHafa said. They fell to the floor together and fireworks started as they fondled each other. She kissed him gently on his forehead and then started kissing him everywhere else. He began taking off more clothes because he was getting way too hot.

"I just love how I feel right now!" A-Rod said, relaxed. "Can we make sweet love like this all the time?"

"Only when I am with you, I can feel this way," NaHafa uttered. "I think we have something golden going, and

I want it to last forever. I have always thought I could feel this way about a man, but never had the right guy in mind, and now I have him!"

"I am so glad all the events happened like they did, or else we would not have ended up together," A-Rod said. They lay together in each other's arms like a happy couple. Later, they ended their rendezvous with a nap together.

* * * *

At this point, JL and Carlos were in control, since Paria had gone to take a nap, as well.

"The both of us will hawk-eye and take that monster, don't you worry, Paria," JL said. "You go and take your nap with no worries, ma'am." Austin, Yao, Manny, BA, and Hay-Hay hung around, awaiting the spaceship's approach. It seemed the ship was closing in faster and faster.

Later, everybody switched roles, making sure that at least four of the BASIC 12 watched the enormous UFO and whatever was lurking inside at all times. Next, Yao, Manny, BA, Hay-Hay, Austin, JL, and Carlos went to their own quarters to take naps.

"I will let you all know if anything changes, people," I said courageously. "Holler at ya' boy."

The alien's spaceship, which I had secretly named The Unicore, was like a James Bond spaceship, it had so many gadgets and tricks up its sleeve. The Untouchable creature inside was looking to take no prisoners, I thought.

Chapter 4

Suddenly, the spaceship disappeared into hyperspace so quickly we almost didn't notice. "Wow! What just happened?" I said. "What was that powerful zoom noise! Where did that strange UFO go?"

"Okay, that did it for me!" Carlos answered. The rest of the BASIC 12 went on full alert, and everyone went to his or her battle stations.

"Warning! Full alert! Report to your pods at once. I repeat; this is a full alert. Please report to you pods at once and that's an order!" the loudspeaker said.

Everyone was fully aware of the UFO in front of us as we made our way to our respective pods. The ship was as close as it had ever been, studying our ship's defenses. I thought, in its disappearance, the UFO was playing yet another trick on us. Then there was a loud BOOM.... then ...

Chapter Five:
The Hexapod and The Untouchable's Collision

Everyone was awakened by the loud BOOM that shook the entire spaceship. "Okay, what the heck was that loud noise?" Manny asked.

"I am not sure, but we intend as a group to find out and investigate what happened," JL added.

Everyone spoke over the intercom from their pods, saying, "Is everything okay out there?"

I added, "Is anybody hurt?"

"A little shaken, but everyone seems to be alright," was the response.

"Then let us go find out what that was!" I added.

"Hey Tevie, who made you the leader? That is my line to the company," JL said.

"I know, but it just shot out of my mouth."

The BASIC 12 looked out into space from each of the six pods and saw nothing in particular. "Hey, where is that monster?" Austin said.

"You know, it is weird, we just had heard a loud boom, yet there's not anything to see," JL said curiously.

Paria and I noticed a dent in the Hexapod that was not there before. Paria marched to her troops and explained what the loud boom was. "Did you see what that UFO did to our

Chapter 5

ship? It dented us good," Paria said angrily. She called everyone to his or her stations to get ready for combat, just to be safe. "Revenge, revenge!" Paria shouted courageously. Then she ordered every pod to release a heat seeker missile into space to defend another attack.

"Is everybody ready?" JL said.

"I am locked in," Carlos answered.

"Are you all sure it is still in front of us?" Yao asked.

"I am not sure, but we are about to find out!" BA replied with certainty.

"Fire away at will!" Paria said. We fired and then a war started.

"Wow, it was there all along," Yao noticed.

The Unicore took a hit and regained its visual existence, firing back at the Hexapod. The Hexapod was able to dodge the first nine attacks from the Unicore, but the Untouchable did not give up. It kept firing solid blasts at us. The war went on for some time, as the Hexapod and the Unicore kept dodging each other's attacks.

Soon, Unicore was badly hit on one of its wings. The BASIC 12 were happy and we applauded and jumped for joy.

"Hooray," said Hay-Hay willingly.

"Hey, don't speak too soon and stay posted," JL added.

"Hey, what is going on with that thing?" Austin said, trembling with fear.

"Yeah, why is its outer shell glowing like that?" Safoya noticed as the Unicore vanished into hyperspace again. We thought we had scared it away.

"I guess we got rid of it, huh?" I said to the company.

"I guess we scared it away, I think," A-Rod said cheerfully.

"I do not know," JL said. "Let us fire some warning shots just to make sure it is gone and not still hanging around."

"I think we are okay!" Paria said to JL.

"Is it okay to cheer now?" Austin added.

"No way," Manny and Hay-Hay said. "We cannot sleep until we know that Untouchable thing and its ship is dead."

The company broke for a while. Yao and BA utilized their mechanical skills and tried to revamp the dent the Unicore left behind. "You see the size of that dent in the ship?" Yao measured it.

"It has to be about four or five feet long," BA guessed.

"Yep, you are about right. Four and a half," she added. "This is really going to take awhile, huh?"

Chapter 5

BA said, "Yes, this will take more than a minute, surely."

Fixing the dent took hours and hours, and some people got hungry while in the midst of a war. So before anything else happened, they all grabbed quick, ready to eat rations.

"Now, I got a good reason to sit down and bite into some delicious baked chicken," Manny noted.

"And what reason is that?" Austin added.

"Well, all this war and battle makes me think too hard and this food will refuel me."

"That is it, refuel and recharge," I said. "That is what that glow around the Unicore was."

"So you mean to tell me a ship can recharge itself?" Carlos questioned.

"I do not know, but to me it is a possibility."

All was well and lunch came to an end. They returned to their battle stations immediately after the meal. Yao and BA went back to the dent in the Hexapod and sealed it off smoothly.

"Okay Paria, we've got this under control," BA said.

"Well, good, now get back to your quarters, so we can lock together as one unit," Paria said.

As we looked into outer space, a glimpse of something caught my eye. Paria saw it too, and soon others did, too.

"Hey, we really need to be ready this time," BA said.

"I've got the feeling it has gotten smarter about how to handle us now," I said.

Another alert went out to make sure everybody had returned to his or her pods and was prepared for battle. Not only had the Unicore gotten smarter, but the BASIC 12 had seen two ships this time.

"Hey, this thing has doubled the trouble tremendously," Carlos realized.

"Hey, it is already hard to fight one of these ships, but now there are two," Austin said.

"What do we do about this situation?" BA said with fear.

The Untouchable was in one ship, and the other was just a decoy to confuse the BASIC 12 about where the monster really was.

"Something fishy is going on here. There's no way there's two monsters, right?" Yao shouted.

"I cannot say, but we do not know what these creatures are capable of," Paria replied.

"They are so alike in every aspect, it seems," JL noted.

The rest of the company watched the ships approach

Chapter 5

rapidly and they could not tell them apart. The Unicore and the decoy ship looked similar in every aspect and the company could not tell which ship was controlling which. I could tell that this Untouchable creature was learning and getting smarter with time.

JL was fascinated. "It is smarter than we think."

Carlos and the rest of us were waiting for something to happen and anxious for Paria to command us to attack. But Paria was trying to figure out what the monster was up to beforehand. What happened next puzzled the BASIC 12, since both ships flew toward the Hexapod at the same time.

"Hey, what is going on? What are those ships doing?" Austin said.

"Company, get locked into position and get ready to fire," Paria said.

The Untouchable was a crafty alien and its reflexes were turning out to be faster than ours. Suddenly, there was a loud booming sound.

"Not another hit," JL said.

"We never got a chance to take a shot at the ship," Safoya added.

The two ships headed toward the Hexapod, causing the Hexapod to change its coordinates.

"Hey Paria, we have lost our coordinate path system," Yao said. "We are officially thrown off course because of this hit."

The Warsan Center was trying to contact the company, but they were in the midst of another attack so they had no time to talk. Austin got tired of watching and he couldn't sit still. Then there was another loud booming sound. "Oh man, what was that?" Austin thought.

Then he said, "We must do something quick, JL. I am really getting scared of this creature."

"You're supposed to be a soldier, so act like one," JL said.

Paria shouted over the intercom, "The loud boom was a heavy object that dropped some distance from the ceiling on the ship."

"I think it was more than that," Austin said. The Untouchable's decoy ship fired missiles at the Hexapod, while the Unicore vanished into hyperspace.

"Man, we might not even be fighting the right ship!" JL noted. "We could be wasting our heavy artillery on a decoy, you know?" he added.

"Well, what do you suggest?" Paria said to him.

"I am not sure!" JL said.

"If we stop firing I believe it will start firing back at us," Paria said.

"I do not want to take that chance either, so I understand," JL said.

Chapter 5

Getting rid of the decoy proved to be harder than they anticipated. It was as if it was being operated by a remote control in hyperspace.

The battle between the Unicore and the Hexapod continued.

"When will this end?" Austin said.

"Yeah, you're right. We cannot fight off this thing forever," NaHafa said. The Hexapod was like an enemy in a video game, the one who was about to be taken down. But we wouldn't give up.

"There must be some monster in that ship, flying that thing with those great maneuvers," JL said.

"If there's no one in that ship, we really have a smart creature on our hands," Paria yelled.

The BASIC 12 fought with everything we had, but the Unicore's decoy dodged our shots better than the Unicore did and this was amazing to JL. "What had we gotten ourselves into?" JL spoke over the intercom. JL found a direct line on the ship and locked in on the target. He was waiting for Paria to give him the okay. "I've got a good shot of getting rid of that wretched monster for good, I think."

Paria was controlling the ship and the Hexapod dodged a few more attacks from the decoy under her control. Then she told JL to fire when he saw fit. JL fired at the decoy's force field defense, found the perfect spot and sent out a blast that destroyed it completely.

This angered the Untouchable and in retaliation, it thrust the decoy ship toward the Hexapod.

"You made that ship mad, it is coming for us really fast," Austin noted. "It's locked in on us and it's coming too fast for us to try to hit it."

"I am about to fire," JL said.

"No, don't!" Paria and Austin said at the same time. But it was too late. JL had already released the missile. The blast blew up the decoy before it got too close, but the impact breached POD 3 severely. Inside the pod, JL and Austin, exploded on impact before the rest of the company could do anything to prevent it.

"Oh no!" said Yao.

"Secure the ship! That's an order," Paria said loudly.

"You all heard the boss, let us do it!" Carlos added.

Each of the remaining pods pushed their security buttons to cut off all connections to the destroyed pod.

"Hey, we must act fast or we will all die soon," Paria yelled.

"Oh, no," Safoya said. "Why us and why those two? Why is all of this happening now?"

"If I had an answer for that I might have been able to prevent it," Paria continued.

At this point, there were only ten of us left. JL and

Chapter 5

Austin had perished in outer space, along with POD 3. The whole company went into mourning, but only for a split second, because the Untouchable was not finished.

I began to understand why I had known bad things were going to happen and how badly I was going to feel because of them. Now I felt even worse, especially since I couldn't really do anything about what was happening. With the decoy destroyed, there were only ten of us left to fight the monster effectively and efficiently. Everything happened so quickly that we'd had little time to react.

"What to do now? One of our leaders is gone and now his kids are fatherless," Safoya said.

"I am not sure at this point, because that ship was breached and destroyed," Paria said.

"Poor young Austin, he was a cadet at heart," NaHafa continued, "Now he is just a memory in heart."

* * * *

The rest of the company and I continued to be in mourning for a while. Time went by and we had to take stress tablets given to us by the robot maids, to keep us going strong. To pay our respects, we set up a candlelight vigil for JL and Austin, and hummed a song for them.

We knew that whatever had come at us before would be back. We had to find ways to out think the Untouchable. Although it seemed like it took forever and a day, we initialized and restored our force field.

"I never knew it could take so long to revamp a ship," Carlos said.

"It is actually a fun thing for me," Yao said. "I am used to fixing up things that are all bent out of shape."

This time Paria gave different commands. She ordered Manny, Yao, BA, and NaHafa to get to work on the force field, while Hay-Hay, Carlos, A-Rod, Safoya, and I each chose a Pod and kept watch for the return of the Unicore.

Manny asked Yao about the men she'd been with. "Why do you seem quiet all the time, ma'am?"

Yao told him, "I am not gay and I like men very much, thank you. I have had my share of men, but they never wanted to be serious. I do not just sleep around all the time, like some people do."

Manny laughed to his heart's content and was content with what she'd said.

NaHafa told them to drop the soap opera drama, since that was over and done with now. "Why are you messing with Yao about her situation with men?" NaHafa added. "We have been through enough drama about that already and that has been over for some time." She started crying. "There are more important things to worry about now, like avenging Austin and JL's death. They should not have had to die. What went wrong? Why is this creature among us?" NaHafa cried out. "If we do not do something, it might kill us all."

BA said, "She is right. We should be working on the force field so we can protect ourselves from this alien and his ship." They worked efficiently to fix the force field.

* * * *

Back at the space station, Paria saw a glimpse of the spaceship again, coming closer and closer. It approached rapidly and then it zoomed to the left and the right, headed for the northeast wing of the Hexapod. Paria ordered them to hurry with the force field.

"Hey, that ship and the monster are on the move. Hurry up with that force field, so we all can get back to our battle stations quickly," Paria shouted. She fired at the Unicore, but it dodged her attack swiftly and moved toward the Pod Hay-Hay was occupying.

"Hay-Hay, it is coming for your side of the ship!" Paria yelled.

"I know, I see it and I'm ready to go at it." Hay-Hay fired his last three heat seekers at the Unicore and they all missed. When he got low on ammo, Paria took cover while he reloaded.

"Hey cadet, the rest of the team will hold this thing off for awhile," Carlos shouted.

Paria could not cover for much longer, since the Unicore was still firing at the Hexapod. Carlos fired shots from the laser cannon, but it did not matter since the Unicore was so amazing with dodge maneuvers. With only eighty percent of the Hexapod left, Paria urged the company to fight harder.

"I need some help!" Paria shouted.

"It is moving in on me too fast! Help!" Hay-Hay added. And before the rest of the team started firing away, they thought about how close the ship had actually gotten.

The Untouchable went into rapid speed and came full blast toward Hay-Hay's pod. With the force field shield down, it was curtains for Hay-Hay. "Hey company, I am going to give this monster all I got. I am reloaded now," he said. "Company, it's too close, way too close!' Although, he did get a good shot in at the Unicore, it was not enough to save his life. The Unicore's beam cut through the seams of the Hexapod and right through Hay-Hay. His pod exploded instantly, shocking the other members. We could not pause for one moment of grief over his death, since we were in the midst of battle.

I was seeing all of this unfolding and I could not do anything about it, except fire shots when Paria told me to. Now I felt grief over the deaths of Austin, JL and Hay-Hay, rage boiled my blood. This menacing creature had to be stopped somehow. The hit caused the Hexapod's wing to collapse and explode, leaving dust and debris floating in outer space before the Unicore floated below the Hexapod at hyper speed. This allowed us more time to finish repairing the force field.

"God help us! What have we done to deserve this treatment, please tell us? Paria whispered. "Hey, let us fix

Chapter 5

that force field shield, why don't we?"

"I am right on it!" BA replied. But it was too late, for the Unicore was getting extremely close.

The Unicore breached the ship from underneath by sneak attack, leaving a large gash in the Hexapod and making a loud noise.

"The creature has crashed into our ship," Safoya said. "I wish our coordinate system was up and running, so that we could pinpoint exactly where he is."

The Unicore made a crash landing underneath the Hexapod. I looked out into outer space and saw nothing. Then, I knew the creature had hit the ship. "What do we do now, boss?" I asked.

Paria was at a loss for words, now that there had been three fatalities on her watch. "I do not know," she said, tearfully.

"We must be strong and survive this," I said. "So come on, what is the next move? Tell me so I can do it."

She started crying like a baby, telling the rest of the company that she hated that Hay-Hay did not survive their last battle. She had flashbacks about how heroic JL was and how much energy Austin had in finding out things. "We must put our thinking caps on. He has killed three of our astronauts and he will not take us all without a fight," she yelled.

"Now this is the Paria I am used to seeing as my

boss!" I said.

"I think there is a hole in the ship now."

The force field would not function properly, since the ship had been hit. Paria ordered Safoya to close off the damaged pod Hay-Hay had been in and our attention shifted to the loud boom we'd all heard. Manny, Yao, BA, and NaHafa went on a search to find the source of the booming noise. Manny checked the basement first and found no hole. Yao went deeper and checked the second level of the basement and there was some debris, but no hole. Nahafa checked the third level of the basement and found the hole. NaHafa investigated a small room nearby, saw nothing out of the ordinary and left it. As she was stepping out, she asked Paria to activate the shutoff mechanism for that room, since too much air was getting out too quickly.

"Is anything down there, any hint or clue?" Paria asked.

"I am looking around boss, but I see nothing strange," NaHafa answered. "I am on my way back to you," NaHafa said.

"Remember what we saw in the binoculars, a slimy liquid creature?" Paria noted. "Maybe there is slime on the walls or the floor?"

"If there was, there is not any now," NaHafa said. "I do not see anything that looks suspicious in that room. I am on my way back, over and out."

Chapter 5

Meanwhile, Paria, still grieving the loss of the three astronauts, dropped roses for them into outer space through an exhaust chute.

* * * *

Because of the hole in the ship, the Hexapod lost some of its altitude and started to cease flying. "I can feel us moving down some, that hole messed up our position," I noted.

We found the engine room next and attempted to fix the damage there, too. BA, who was already there, said, "We are losing attitude fast."

"No duh!" I said quickly.

"Come on company, no time for games," Paria shouted. "We must act fast or this creature will be the last thing we see!" She had no way of knowing that the Untouchable was already on board.

"Do you think that creature is on this ship?" BA uttered.

"I am not sure. I do not know the position of the ship," I said. "But we cannot mourn forever. We must apply the correct defense to beat this thing." We all knew something was fishy about the hole and the area where the hole was, but we couldn't pinpoint what it was.

Meanwhile, the Untouchable hid himself in a closet along the corridor in the basement. It was waiting until everything calmed down in time and then it would make its move.

Paria felt so badly about the deaths of her most heroic soldiers that she did not know what to do or say. "I am so mad at myself. As your commander I am ashamed. I was so helpless through all of this catastrophe," she wept.

"It is not your fault!" I mentioned.

"Yeah, boss, some things we really have no control over," Safoya added.

"I know we all feel badly about the deaths of our cadets, but we must get our minds set to go back home and be a witness to what we saw," BA said.

The rest of the company was scattered about the Hexapod, mourning in their own private ways and becoming angry at the creature.

"I hate to see our boss cry so much. We must destroy this creature," I said to BA.

"Okay, cadet, what is your strategy?" BA questioned.

"I am not sure yet. I cannot rush into suggesting options without thinking or I just might get us killed," I told him. "If we are going to beat this thing we must beat it at its own game."

"I hear you, but talk is like two cents. Cheap," BA responded.

Unfortunately, the Untouchable was much too clever. It cut the power cords to the ship's satellite, which was the

Chapter 5

frequency used to communicate with Earth and the Warsan Center.

Paria warned everyone. "Everyone, our communication to Warsan Avionics Center is lost. Do not panic, we must be strong and survive this thing," she added. She called another meeting at the round table and the question everyone wanted to ask but didn't, eventually came up.

"Is that monster on this ship?" Safoya asked.

"I am not sure yet, but I think so," I responded.

"And exactly how do you know?" BA asked me.

"Well, considering all the events that have happened and the fact that everything has calmed down a bit, I think our arch enemy is hiding somewhere on this ship. But then again, I could be wrong."

"Well, I refuse to allow that monster to keep me stressed out forever," BA said.

"He is right," Safoya replied. "We must go at this thing before it comes at us. I'm still scared though."

"That thing could be plotting on us and we do not even know it," BA said to me.

All that was left of our regiment, in order of command, were Paria, Carlos, Yao, Manny, Safoya, A-Rod, Na-Hafa, BA, and me. I was last in command but it seemed like I was the one with all the great ideas. At the same time, I was enraged and I wanted the alien to show itself, so I could kill it or at least find a weakness to contain it. I would even sacrifice my life to make sure the creature was destroyed and would not travel back to Earth with us.

All was quiet and the round table meeting lasted about thirteen hours. Before it concluded, we prayed for our safety, even though we did not pray much on the ship. And shortly after we prayed, the drama only got worse.

Chapter Six:
Fatal Drama

"We need to start making some moves on this creature. What are we waiting on boss?" Manny said.

"What is our next move?" BA said to the crew. He was becoming impatient and so was the Untouchable.

The Untouchable left his hiding place in the closet and moved swiftly in the direction of the gym, his tentacles floating in the air behind him. There it hid for hours, swimming in the pool and holding himself comfortably underwater and waiting until the time was right.

I began to suspect that there was something suspicious going on, but I knew not what. I noticed that the Unicore's coordinates hadn't moved since we had placed markers on our screen to track its movement. Paria made note of this in her tablet and alerted the others via walkie-talkie, telling us to get ready for battle.

"You heard your boss, everybody. Let's get to our spots!" Carlos remarked.

"You ain't gotta tell me twice," BA responded vengefully.

Safoya said, "Yes, finally we're going at this creature.

"I hope we get rid of this thing once and for all," Yao added. "We will. Yes, we will," Manny said.

Chapter 6

"Don't worry, my rage will take over in this battle!" I said courageously. "Fire heat-seeker one."

"Tevie, who put you in charge?" Carlos said angrily. I was overriding Paria's command to hold fire.

I ignored him and fired at the Unicore to knock it back. Then I fired numerous shots and blew a hole in the Unicore.

"Hey Tevie, why override my authority?" Paria said.

"Hey look, the ship has been hit and hit well," Safoya noted.

"Never mind what I said," Paria continued. "But we going to have to work on your anger management later."

"Hey, keep firing, we should be able to destroy it if we keep firing to knock it back some more," Yao explained.

"You ain't saying nothing but a word," BA said.

"Keep firing at will," Paria noted.

We finished off the Unicore quickly by hitting it with a sonic blast. "Yes! We defeated that thing and we need to celebrate, for real," BA said.

"I would not celebrate just yet," I noted.

"Tevie is right. How do we know we killed the monster or whatever that was we saw through those binoculars?" Safoya replied. "I am just glad that ship is no more and now we can figure out how to get back home."

"I've done away with the bothersome UFO and nobody really had to help me," I shouted happily. The company rejoiced, praising my efforts. "I do not need this honor. I am just glad we are all still alive."

"Can we start marching back to Earth now, please?" Manny said with cheer.

Although the Unicore was gone, I did not understand why it had been so easy to destroy it considering what we had been through before. I couldn't help thinking that this was all a hoax and that the alien was still lurking about somewhere. I still felt uneasy.

* * * *

The Untouchable felt the vibration from the explosion of the Unicore and became even angrier with the Earthlings. He was plotting his attack while we were celebrating his demise. We drank wine and ate lots of food to celebrate his destruction, and most of the company got drunk. We began to feel drowsy and tired.

"I want to go and take a swim and relax," Manny said to the group. "I've got swim trunks the girls might love to see."

"Nobody cares about seeing you in your trunks," Safoya added.

"I can see why you would say that and it is understandable," Manny uttered back.

"Okay you all, cool it. This is no time to bring up the

Chapter 6

past," Paria said. "Besides, we've got bigger fish to fry and bigger situations to deal with. Manny, go take your swim and relax."

Manny went to the gym and took a shower in the shower room. Then he went into the sauna before heading to the pool.

He was not aware of the danger in the deep end of the pool. The Untouchable's tentacles felt the vibration of the water when Manny jumped in. He stayed hidden while Manny swam for hours, doing butterfly tricks and playing around in the water. When he grew tired, he decided to get out of the pool. The Untouchable swam quickly from the deepest points of the water toward Manny. As Manny stepped onto the stairs to climb out, the Untouchable stretched out its long tentacles and pulled him back in forcefully.

"Help! Someone help me, please!" he shouted. "Someone please help me, I am under attack!"

The monster cut off Manny's head first with its sharp tentacles, then his arms and legs. Manny died instantly. What was left of his bloody body sank to the depths of the pool. It pierced Manny's corpse with its egg-producing tentacles, but the change he was hoping for did not occur. Manny's body would have to be disposed of in another way. It climbed out of the pool, left the first gymnasium and headed for the second gymnasium, moving swiftly and silently.

BA left the celebration early and was already in the second gymnasium shooting free throws and working on his basketball techniques. While shooting a free throw, the Untouchable crept into to the second gym and sneaked over to BA, stealing the basketball from him quickly. The monster ran with it toward another part of the gym.

BA was shocked at what he had seen. "Help!" he screamed, racing over to the security button as fast as he could. "Help! Help! Can anyone hear through these vents?" BA shouted.

It was unfortunate there were no intercoms in any of the gyms, just emergency security buttons. The Untouchable dashed across the room with its tentacles out and cut off BA's legs. BA fell to the hardwood floor, blood squirting everywhere. The Untouchable walked up to BA and stood over him.

"Why would you do this to me?" BA said tearfully, in pain. "What have I done to make you attack me like this?"

The creature used his many tentacles to smack BA's head around a few times while he was still alive. He fought his way loose and tried to slide across the floor to the security button. But the Untouchable finished him off quickly, jumping up into the air and landing on his head, instantly smashing him. The Untouchable stuck its egg-producing tentacles in BA, hoping to see some type of change. There was no change and he was puzzled first and then angry. He collected both bodies and hid them in a nearby closet.

* * * *

Back at the celebration extravaganza, Paria was keeping up with attendance and wanting to know where every-

Chapter 6

one was. "Okay, some hours have passed and some people have not returned."

"Yeah, that is kind of odd, considering that after BA has a good workout he usually wants some good food to eat," Safoya said.

"He should have made it back by now," Paria said. She went over to the loudspeaker and put out a call for everyone to check in.

"I reckon so, and Manny should have, as well," Safoya added.

Carlos and Yao had left the party to go and play some board games, and A-Rod, NaHafa and I had gone to our quarters to relax.

"Hey, something must be wrong if Paria is yelling at us over the intercom," A-Rod told NaHafa.

"There might be. Let's go check it out," NaHafa responded.

"Oh man, just when I was about to get some rest, the boss has to call a meeting," I said to myself as I prepared to respond to Paria's call.

She heard back from all of the cadets except two, Manny and BA. "Hey BA and Manny, where are you?" Paria yelled. "Hey Manny and BA answer your walkie-talkies now! That's an order!" There was no answer from either of them and she knew something was wrong. She called a meeting and ordered everyone to attend. Only Carlos, Yao,

Safoya, Alex, NaHafa, and I showed.

"What happened to the rest of our team?" Carlos asked. "Anybody got any ideas where else they could have gone on the ship?"

"All we know is what he told us," Safoya said.

"Well, obviously we need to form a type of search party and find them immediately!" Carlos said with certainty.

Paria was not sure where they were, but she knew she had called them and they hadn't responded. We split up into teams and searched for Manny and BA in every nook and cranny of the spaceship. Paria had ordered us to report for another safety check, in eight hours.

Paria went to the gym first, because she knew BA loved basketball. "Hey cadet! Are you around?" Paria yelled loudly. "Holler if you hear me, cadet!" There was no answer in the gym, only the echoes of her voice over and over again. She found BA's basketball still by the basketball goal. "This is definitely BA's basketball, because his initials are engraved on it." She picked up the ball and bounced it a few times as she thought about what it might mean. He was never without his basketball if he could help it.

Paria walked into the shower room and found the water running, but no one there. There was something dark smudged on the wall. "Huh, what is that crap on the wall over there?" she said as she walked closer to turn the water off. "Why would the water still be running and no one is

Chapter 6

around? Manny, BA, are you guys in here?"

Then she heard a creepy, crawling sound. She looked around and saw nothing out of the ordinary, even though the hair on the back of her neck was standing up. A few seconds later, she felt warm liquid on her shoulders. She looked at it and gasped. "Oh no, where is this blood coming from?" She looked up at the ceiling and screamed in disgust as she saw Manny's corpse. The impact of the scream was so jarring that the corpse dropped from the ceiling and fell on her. "Help! Someone help! Please come quick!" She took one last look at Manny before freeing herself from his body weight. "Oh no, Manny, poor Manny. Who would do such a thing to you?"

Paria stood as fast as she could, intent on checking the other shower rooms, but the Untouchable had other plans for her. Just before she would've crossed the threshold he made his move. Suddenly, he burst through a wall on the other side of the shower room and stopped her from getting away. He flew across the room toward her with his tentacles coiled in anticipation. One encircled Paria's neck and a few seconds later her neck was broken. Two of his other tentacles ripped her arms and legs from her body.

Just as he had done the others, the Untouchable pierced Paria's body with a tentacle and waited for something to happen. Instead of dying like the others, Paria fell into a deep sleep. Later, she would awaken with a racing heart and a new existence, more like that of the Untouchable. Because Paria's corpse was of a different species, his egg-producing injection was successful on her. The parasite he had just planted in her would feed off of her and would eventually take over her body. It would become like him.

* * * *

In another part of the ship, Carlos was still trying to find BA and Manny. He checked the ship's main level and didn't find anything, then he used the intercom. "Hey, Manny and BA, where are you two hiding?" he said. "Please give us your location so this search party can end! Yao, any luck?"

"None here boss," Yao answered back over the intercom. Yao had checked the rear parts of the ship, with no luck either. "Hey, Manny and BA, where are you, my fellow cadets?" she called out. She saw an intercom in a nearby corridor and used it to try contacting Paria. "Paria, are you there?" Static was her only response.

After hours of searching, Yao started to get hungry so she went to the cafeteria. The first thing she noticed when she arrived was that food was strewn all over the place, some of it half-eaten. She used the kitchen intercom to call Carlos. Something fishy was going on. "Hey, Carlos, are you there?" she shouted over the intercom.

"Yes, what's up?" he responded.

"No food, that is what is up!" Yao continued, "All of our food has been consumed and or wasted. I repeat, all of our food has been consumed."

"What? What the heck?" Carlos said.

Chapter 6

"If we do not find some food soon, we all might die of starvation later," Yao said.

"Oh no, I must start heading back that way toward you," Carlos said.

"What did you say?" Yao asked as they began losing their connection frequency up between Carlos and Yao. She left the intercom and went back to the refrigerator. "I must find something to eat." She was so hungry she was beginning to forget who she was. Hours went by while Yao tried to call another cadet over the intercom and her walkie-talkie, but neither was working properly. She sat there for a while, thinking about how delicious a chicken sandwich would be to her taste buds.

Chapter Seven:
The Baby Untouchable is Born

While the rest of the company was still scrambling to discover the whereabouts of Manny and BA, Paria died in human spirit and returned to life in the form of an Untouchable. The creature lurking inside of Paria was using her blood to grow at an alarming rate. Sooner than the Untouchable had anticipated, Paria's transformation was complete. The baby Untouchable burst out of Paria's chest and stomach with superhuman strength. It smelled BA's corpse, left Paria's corpse and went to nibble on BA ravenously. It went into hiding shortly thereafter, while it got acclimated to its new surroundings and continued to grow.

In another part of the damaged Hexapod, Carlos left the upper level, headed for the mid-level to continue searching. "Manny, BA, where are you?" Carlos yelled. His voiced echoed down the corridor.

Yao eventually found a box of candy bars in the closet next to the one hiding BA's corpse. "This is good stuff here," Yao said, smacking loudly. "It is about time I found some good food." She found more food in the gym. "Wow, I must have been searching the wrong spots. Seems like all or most of the goodies are here. But, why?" she said to herself as she started eating like she was dying of starvation.

She looked down and saw fresh blood leaking out of the closet BA was in. "Huh what, what is this?" she noticed something red on the floor. "Is that blood?" she asked

Chapter 7

the empty room. "I wonder where it's coming from?" She opened the closet door slowly and saw BA's body, chopped into pieces. "Oh no! Help!" She threw up and started crying.

She ran to the other end of the gym, where a security button was, but it had been destroyed. Then she heard noise coming from the shower room and went to see what was going on. There, she found what was left of Paria's mutilated body.

"Oh no, Poor Paria. Where are your legs and arms? Why are people dying like this?" She saw something move out of the corner of her eye and turned to see what it was. "Hey, come here, where are you going? I know you are in here, I can almost smell you." The baby Untouchable crept around the corner and she grabbed it, beating it until greenish-yellow blood spilled from its body.

Afterward, she sat there mourning the deaths of all the fallen cadets. "Why are all these deaths happening to our people? Why us? How will I explain this to the American presses? she wondered.

* * * *

Safoya, A-Rod, NaHafa and I stayed close to the pods during our search for Manny and BA. "I wonder how everybody is fairing on the search," NaHafa said.

"I am sure everything is okay, we just need to stay close to each other," A-Rod said.

"Aw, just like two lovebirds, look at y'all!" I said to them.

"Are y'all sure they are okay?" Safoya noted. "I mean they really have been gone for some time, wouldn't you say?"

"Okay, let's try to radio them," A-Rod said and tried to adjust the frequency on his walkie-talkie. "It will not go through, the frequency must be broken."

"Try again," Safoya said.

"Okay, okay, hold your horses!" A-Rod said. "The security intercom is not working properly either."

Carlos was headed to the ship's entertainment area when he encountered the Untouchable. On his way down the corridor to the disco area, the Untouchable burst through the wall directly in front of him and blocked his path.

"What the...?" he said. "I cannot believe it, you are the monster we saw in the binoculars!" Armed with a loaded special gun, he wasted no time shooting the Untouchable. But the bullets were barely making a dent in the monster's bulk.

The Untouchable picked Carlos up with its tentacles and shook him so hard all of his ammunition fell to the floor. Then he tossed Carlos up in the air so fast he got dizzy and his nose started bleeding. Seconds later, Carlos went soaring through the ceiling, into the upper level.

"If I want to live, I must get up and hide myself!" he

Chapter 7

said to himself. "I hurt so badly. Ouch, ouch!"

The Untouchable followed Carlos through the ceiling, planning to finish him off, but Carlos was nowhere in sight. Surprised, the monster stood there looking around the empty room. Carlos caught him off guard when he popped out of his hiding place with a lead pipe and slammed it over his head, but his actions didn't do any good. The pipe bent like cheap metal.

"This thing must have a weakness! It must!" Carlos said as he took off running down the corridor. The Untouchable's tentacles shot out and wrapped around Carlos' legs, snapping them off before Carlos realized what was happening. Because Carlos was a male, no change occurred when his body was pierced by the Untouchable's tentacle. Carlos screamed from the pain and forced the monster to decapitate him to quiet the noise.

* * * *

Everyone else was still searching for BA and Manny, but Yao already knew what had happened to them. She found a security button that hadn't been destroyed and pushed it hopefully.

"Did you hear that?" said A-Rod.

"Yes, I did, homie!" I said.

"Let us get ready to go and see!" Safoya noted.

But as soon as Yao pushed the security button, the Untouchable raced in her direction. His feet left the ground as he flew at her with his tentacles out, slicing her body in half at the waist. Before the company could get to her, she was dragged into a nearby closet and pierced by a tentacle. By the time the Untouchable left her there was parasite feeding off of her from the inside out, preparing to transform into another baby Untouchable.

* * * *

Hours later, Carlos's corpse was spotted on a video camera in the hallway of the third floor, so Safoya and A-Rod went to check it out. "Hey, I think something happened to Carlos. Look at this!" Safoya noted.

NaHafa and I stayed in the front pods. "Do you think Carlos is okay?" I said.

"I do not know, Tevie. He looked pretty bad lying there!" NaHafa noted.

When Safoya and A-Rod located the spot where they had seen Carlos's corpse on the video camera, it and the blood it was lying in was gone.

"Okay, I know this is where we saw it," A-Rod said.

"This is crazy, there is the camera right there," Safoya said. "What is going on, A-Rod?"

"I do not know, but there's something wrong here, for sure!"

* * * *

Back at the pod center, NaHafa said, "I am scared

Chapter 7

stiff and I need to be next to a man right now."

I told her, "Hang in there. We will need all our strength, courage, and awareness to get through this alive."

"Hey, we are so worried about Carlos now, but where are BA, Manny, Paria, and Yao?" NaHafa continued, "We need to radio some of the others to find out what is going on!"

I responded, "I hear ya lady, we will get to those people, too."

* * * *

The Untouchable checked on the development of the offspring growing in Yao's body. Yao's corpse was deteriorating and changing colors from blood loss, but the baby was ready to burst forward.

Chapter Eight:
The Final Four

The remaining company found Carlos's corpse in an upper level closet, with his legs and arms lying right beside him. They all cried in disgust and NaHafa vomited all over the floor at her feet. They held hands and prayed.

"My poor Carlos," Safoya said.

"It is such a shame our voyage turned out this way," A-Rod added. "We came on this thing to find new things and we found new life alright! Why did we even encounter this thing? I wish the creature had missed us or something. Maybe, just maybe, we all would be still alive, eating in the conference room!"

"Okay, I know it is good to dream, but we must come back to reality now!" I said quickly. "That thing must die. That thing is on the ship hiding somewhere and we need to find it. We need to find out where Yao is and notify her about Carlos's death, too. I am in mourning and scared just like the rest of you, but we have to find a way to defeat this creature before it gets us all. We do not know how many this monster has taken out already, but one thing is for certain, we must beat this creature and get this ship to safety soon."

In the shower room, NaHafa, A-Rod and Safoya found Paria's mangled corpse. "I do not know how much more of this I can take," Safoya said, crying.

"Me, either," NaHafa said, crying too.

Chapter 8

"I cannot believe that it's only us left!" I said.

"That thing has taken out eight people already!" Na-Hafa said. "I am so scared for us now, A-Rod!"

"See, that is what it wants, you to be scared of it so it can kill you easily," I said. "We need a plan and we must have courage to go up against that thing!"

* * * *

Manny was found immersed in his own blood and cut into pieces. And since there was no sign of Yao anywhere on the ship, we assumed she was dead, too. I noticed that the male bodies had been cut up, but the women's bodies had been mutilated almost beyond recognition. "I do not know if you guys noticed, but I noticed how Paria's stomach was blown out and none of the male bodies were." There had to be something different about the women the monster encountered versus the men. Apparently, it did not treat ladies very nicely, at all.

Safoya asked, "Where in the ship would Yao be?"

I replied, "We looked on each of the floors and in the closets, but no sign of Yao. There were no clues or tips to tell us where she might be, either."

"You think she might be…dead?" Safoya said.

"Well, that is what me and A-Rod are assuming at this point, and you should do the same!" I said.

"Okay, but it will not be easy!" Safoya answered.

"Who said it would be easy? It is not easy for me to say it.

Safoya, NaHafa, A-Rod, and I were the final four on the voyage. We tried to get the Hexapod back into shape by disposing of the corpses. NaHafa and Safoya washed windows and scrubbed the shower rooms, while A-Rod and I picked up bones and fixed holes in the walls.

I was still puzzled by the fact that so many of us had died so quickly. I told the others what we already suspected. Something terrible was on the ship.

NaHafa told me, "Calm down, calm down, right now."

A-Rod told me, "Let's do a final search."

So we did.

* * * *

NaHafa felt uneasy. She told us she was going to the restroom and we all watched her go. Once NaHafa reached the restroom and settled her nerves, she felt better. She emptied her bladder and then went to the vanity to wash her hands. She didn't see the Untouchable creeping up behind her at the sink. She saw it behind her in the mirror.

"Huh? Hey, what the heck?" she said. "Help! Let me get the heck outta here!" She swung her arm back and hit the creature hard, actually hurting the Untouchable and causing it to run away in fear. NaHafa ran out of the restroom, scared.

Chapter 8

Meanwhile, back at the ship's main station, Safoya set the spaceship to auto pilot and went to see why NaHafa was screaming in the restroom. "Hey, NaHafa, are you in there?" Safoya said cautiously, gripping a piece of pipe in her hand.

NaHafa said, "Over here!"

"What are you doing hiding in a corner of the bathroom?"

"I saw it! I saw it!" NaHafa said. "I think it was scared of me, but I was scared of it, too!"

"What did it look like?"

"It was just like the monster we saw through Tevie's binoculars and, in fact, it was identical, I think. It had ugly, slimy tentacles!"

Safoya wanted to believe her story so much, she looked around to see if the monster NaHafa was describing was still there. "I do not see the monster out in the corridor now. It must have fled."

"Please do not leave me alone!" NaHafa begged. "That thing frightens me. I would hate to encounter it again."

"Okay, let us go now. Let's go find the men."

The final four made a pact to stick together for the rest of the voyage, no matter what. We didn't know exactly what happened to the rest of our crew, but we knew that all of them were dead and neither of us wanted to be next. We decided to turn the ship around and head back to Earth.

"Hey, we're getting close to earth. There is our moon!" A-Rod noted.

"Great, that means we are almost home." NaHafa said.

"Hey company, we got work to do!" A-Rod said. "We must apprehend this monster and find a way to land safely soon."

"I wish we could tell someone on Earth about this creature!" NaHafa said.

"We have no frequency right now and our coordinate system seems forever lost!" A-Rod noted.

Despite our pact to stick together at all times, I wanted to take a stroll around the perimeter alone and I did. I marched down to the gym, still curious about that deep water. There I heard a sound. "What was that?" I shot in the direction of the sound, and then I advanced to the acrobat practice section of the gym. Minutes later, the Untouchable followed me. "Alright, no more playing games," I said as I quickly turned around and fired my gun. The first bullet hit my target and I kept shooting. "I guess you were not ready for that, huh?" I said to the creature. I tried to radio the others, but the Untouchable had blocked my frequency. His tentacles came at me fast, but I knocked them away with the pipe in my other hand. I circled around to the door and ran out of the room.

Chapter 8

I met back up with the crowd and told NaHafa that I believed her even more now, because I had seen the monster for myself A-Rod jumped to his feet and was eager to take the monster out, but I told him we needed to wait.

"It is too big and dangerous," I uttered. I'm not sure how I was able to hit it, but it doesn't matter at this point because it did not die. It took all ten of my shotgun blasts. I think it is fool proof. It can probably take on anything right now.

"Let us go get it, for it is only one, but we are four!" A-Rod said smoothly.

"You do not know how dangerous and ugly this creature is!"

"I know enough to know that he is responsible for the deaths of eight cadets!" A-Rod said vengefully.

As a group, we set out to kill the monster.

"You ready to take this thing down, playa?" I said to A-Rod.

"More than you know, homes!" A-Rod replied anxiously.

"But you have not seen that thing first hand," I told A-Rod.

"All I am thinking about is the deaths of our fallen comrades when I am after this thing, but what are you thinking about?"

"Hmm, I guess nothing!"

"The gym is where you saw it right?" A-Rod asked.

"Yes indeed, that is where it was chilling the last time I shot at it," I said.

"Okay I know we're only four people, but we've got enough ammo to take out a small army!" A-Rod said confidently.

"I understand your feelings on this, trust me, playa!" I said.

We retraced my steps back to the gym and tried to call out the Untouchable.

"Where are you, you crazy, ugly beast?" I asked.

"Come out, come out wherever you are! We've got something for you!" NaHafa said.

There was no response and all was silent in the gym. "Okay, Tevie, if you shot the creature it should be hiding, but where?" A-Rod said.

"I do not know," I said.

* * * *

While we were in the gym, the Untouchable crept to the ship's control panel and set the ship to hyperspace mode. We felt the Hexapod moving at high speed.

"Hey, what's going on?" A-Rod said.

Chapter 8

"Someone is controlling the ship!" I said.

"Okay, if we are all here, who is controlling the ship?" NaHafa said.

"Not that creature!" Safoya said with fear.

"Let us go back to the control panel now!" A-Rod shouted. Now we knew where the Untouchable was.

As we marched toward the pod it was in, it closed and locked the door.

"Hey, it is closing the door on us!" Safoya noticed.

"Oh no, how smart is this creature?" A-Rod yelled. We tried to run for the other three doors, but it reconfigured the controls to shut and lock the other three doors, too. "Can anybody tell me what we are dealing with?" A-Rod sounded. "This creature thinks like us. We've got an intelligent monster on our hands."

Instead of blowing the door off, we went in search of the backup generator and control panel. We didn't know that the Untouchable was following us.

"Now I guess we can get that pod door open now, huh?" A-Rod said.

"We just need to hit a few switches and that's it!" Safoya said.

"Hey, did y'all hear that?" I said.

"Hear what?" A-Rod said.

"It was the same creepy sound I heard when I first saw the monster!" I said to A-Rod.

"Hey, there it is over there!" Nahafa said.

"Oh my gosh, it is huge! Fire away at will!" A-Rod said.

"Hey A-Rod, what the heck are you doing?" I said.

"I am avenging my fellow comrades' deaths!" A-Rod charged at the creature with a pointed spear and a shotgun ready.

"Hey A-Rod, get back from that creature!" I said.

A-Rod fired twelve rounds at the creature, but it only stood there yawning, as if it was bored. NaHafa ran from the generator room, scared, and I followed her to make sure she was safe. The action would get heavy not long after.

Chapter Nine:
Tevie Versus The Untouchable

A-Rod continued to throw all he had at the creature, while Safoya watched in amazement. A-Rod yelled for her to help him and she sprang into action.

"Take that and that and that!" she said, firing her pistol.

"I do not think our weapons are doing the job!" A-Rod noted. "We need some other method of destroying this creature, but for now I think our bullets can hold it off." Nothing could stop the creature, it seemed. He threw a pipe at the monster and the monster caught it and threw it right back. It penetrated A-Rod's thigh and he screamed.

"Are you alright?" Safoya said.

"I think the pipe is stuck in my leg!" A-Rod said.

"What? Let us see if we can get it out!"

"No! Save yourself! Run!"

Safoya rejected his words and fired her ammo at the monster, hoping to give A-Rod enough to get the pipe out of his leg so they could make a run for it. But the Untouchable had other ideas. He continued deflecting shots as he got closer to A-Rod. His tentacles uncoiled, snapped A-Rod's neck and sliced A-Rod's body in half. His blood oozed out quickly and A-Rod died instantly.

Safoya screamed at the top of her lungs and ran into

Chapter 9

the entertainment room to get away from the creature. The Untouchable was swift though, rushing behind her with its tentacles out. When he was close enough he sliced her head off, dropping her quickly and splattering blood everywhere. She too was pierced by a tentacle and injected with a blood sucking parasite that would soon birth itself.

I figured out how to unlock the security sub-spaceship attached to the Hexapod. NaHafa was with me. "We really should have stayed back there and fought with them," I said to Nahafa.

"I know, but I am so scared of that monstrous creature!" NaHafa said.

"I think I know the emergency coordinates to release the Hexapod sub-spaceship," I said.

"Great! Let's get the heck outta here!" NaHafa said joyfully.

"Go to the shower room and pick up a wrench. I think we're going to need it."

"I'm scared, Tevie."

"I'll go then," I told her as I gathered ammunition to take with me in case the Untouchable tried to attack me. I told her to lock the door and not to come out of the pod. I walked the corridors of the damaged Hexapod back to the gym area. Green ooze filled the pool and a strange noise filled the room. "What the heck did that creature do?" I said to myself. "The whole pool is green now and what the heck is that funny noise?" It sounded like a baby pup was crying.

Then, in the mirrored acrobat section of the gym, I saw it. It looked just like the Untouchable, only smaller. "Aw, just look at the poor baby!" I said evilly. "I'm so glad I came down here, because now I've got something to waste these bullets on!"

It snapped at me and I jumped back. Then it charged me and I shot it, the bullet grazing its head. I was still shooting when it crashed through the mirrored wall, running away from me.

"Hey, where are you going? Don't you want to come back and play with my little friend?" I said fearlessly. I followed it, still shooting, but the bullets bounced off of him. Suddenly, it turned on me and ran toward me, forcing me to retrace my steps and jump back through the wall. Back in the gym, I shot it again, this time doing more damage. What happened next surprised me. I stopped shooting long enough to stare at the tiny monster, confused as to why it was running around the room smashing all the mirrors. "Oh no you don't!" I said. "Why are you breaking all the mirrors?" The creature managed to break all the mirrors in the room before I finished him off. For my finale, I stuck a grenade in its mouth. "I do not know where the heck you came from, but you're fixing to blow up outta here, playa! Here is something for you to chew on!"

Seconds later, the creature exploded, splattering red and green ooze everywhere. As I covered my face from the

Chapter 9

blast, something occurred to me. The baby creature had revealed something important to me, the Untouchable's weakness. "A mirror image of itself," I murmured. "That's it, that's it! That explains why it ran out of the room." Putting two and two together, I figured out that if the Untouchable was around mirrors, it diminished his powers, making him more human and easily defeated.

I ran back to NaHafa to tell her what I'd figured out. "Hey, lady!" I said.

"What happened? I heard shooting through the vents!" NaHafa noted.

"I think I know the creature's weakness!"

"Really?"

"Yes, ma'am."

"You need to see if A-Rod and Safoya are okay!" NaHafa said. "I felt bad about running away from them and this monster you are talking about, but it scared me."

"Stop being such a weakling about this!" I said firmly.

"I am just fine right here, you go and see about our fellow comrades, okay?" she said.

"Alright, but do not leave from this area!" I told her. "They should be saving themselves, really! Now I know why I've felt so badly throughout this trip." I looked for our comrades and eventually found their remains. They were dead, beyond saving, so I set out to save the final two, NaHafa and myself.

* * * *

I turned one of the security sub-ships, the one carrying me and NaHafa, toward Earth, and put a time bomb on the other one, setting it to detonate hours from now, when we'd be far away from it.

Meanwhile, The Untouchable nursed its young corpse, which was growing by the hour. I had everything in place for our departure, except that I needed to lure the Untouchable to the farthest part of the ship. I wanted him in the emergency meeting room, where I had installed the bomb and insulated it in between the rug and walls, so that, if anyone or anything touched it, it would explode on impact.

"I do not think that ugly creature can see us, just feel our movements," I said to NaHafa.

"How do you know, Tevie?" NaHafa said.

"I do not know! I just had a hunch," I replied. "Okay, it has been a while since we've encountered it and it's pretty quiet down the corridor. It's probably down there nursing his children. I think it creates offspring from human females."

"What? You mean to tell me that ugly monster has sex with people?" NaHafa asked.

"Not exactly, my dear, but it might use some test mechanism on its body," I told her. "I think I just killed its son."

Chapter 9

"You mean there are more of those on this ship?" NaHafa ran into a corner, scared.

"I do not know how many are left, but I know the creature has been studying humans." I explained to her what I'd learned as a result of everyone else's deaths. I realized that to win this battle, we had to outsmart the Untouchable. While we were trying to beat it or him or whatever it was physically, it was winning us over mentally. We needed to work smarter, not harder.

"Let us start the spaceship to take off in ten minutes," I told NaHafa.

While she set the controls, I went to find the vicious monster myself. I went around to each bathroom and pulled mirrors off walls, breaking them and gluing pieces to myself. My goal was to lure him into the emergency meeting room and blow him away.

I called the monster out through the vents. "Come out, come out wherever you are, you numskull!"

The Untouchable made an appearance by breaking five walls to get to me. I hid behind a pillar on the floor until it was in front of me. Then I ran up to him covered in mirror pieces, pulled a shotgun from behind my back and blasted away. It grabbed me with its slimy tentacles and body slammed me, bouncing me against the floor until many of the mirror pieces fell off. It slapped me across the mouth and I hit the floor again, hard. I could see it starting to glow like it was regaining its power and I crawled for my gun. I shot the creature in its power tentacle side and watched it fall through the wall. Then I rose and kept firing until all of my rounds were gone. Thankfully, he landed in the emergency meeting room, where the bomb was, because I was out of ammo.

I ran back to the pod and pushed the ship's self-destruct button. I set it to explode in thirty minutes, and then I hopped onto the security sub-ship with NaHafa. NaHafa was overjoyed that we were finally heading home.

"How come you did not want to fight the creature with me?" I said.

"You knew how scared I was!" NaHafa said to me.

"We could've beat that creature sooner if I'd had some help!" I said.

As we headed for Earth, NaHafa and I mourned the loss of our fallen comrades. We hadn't counted on the Untouchable seeing our ship and going to the Hexapod's main control room to send a missile our way.

"Oh no, NaHafa!" I said. "I think we were hit! That genius of a creature fixed the jam in the main control room and fired at us!"

"What can we do?"

"We must make sure we make a safe landing," I shouted. The ship was going down fast, headed straight for Earth. The closer we got to our home planet, the clearer our communication frequency became.

Chapter 9

"Help! Anybody there, over?" NaHafa said into the speaker.

The Warsan Canter picked up our signal. "We've got your signal, are you there?" the Big Boss responded from the center. Then the Untouchable smashed the frequency system from the main ship. I tapped Morse Code to the Warsan Center, from our sub-ship. I told them of the crash landing we would soon need to make.

The Untouchable figured out that the Hexapod was set to blow up and it overrode the command somehow, freezing the countdown. Then, he sent the baby Untouchable off into outer space in another sub-ship. He pointed the Hexapod toward Earth and followed our ship to a desert in Africa.

"Okay, it is on my turf now and I must deal with this creature once and for all! You ready to see this?"

"Better you than me. Go for it!" NaHafa said.

I was eager to go one on one with the creature. The Warsan Center received notification that the alien had landed on Earth and armed forces stationed in Africa soon surrounded our location.

The battle started. I ran at the Untouchable with all my might, angry all over again about the deaths of my comrades. It rose off the floor with its tentacles flat out in the air. I was strong enough to wrap one of its tentacles around a pillar nearby and stab it with my knife. Then the Untouchable grew the angriest I had ever seen him. It broke lose from the pillar and charged me like a wild bull.

I was so tired from fighting that I could barely move my arms to swing anymore. But I stuck it out and rose to my feet once again, limping toward my gun. I pulled out a spear gun, pointed it at the monster and shot it. The spear went deep into the creature and threw its body to the ground, pinning it there. I pulled out the last hand grenade and C4 I had left.

"Look at all the deaths that you have caused and you've got me working this hard to get rid of you!" I taped and insulated the C4 against the ground where the Untouchable lay and attached the grenade to one of its tentacles. Certain he was trapped, I went back to the ship for NaHafa. We needed to get out of harm's way

"I saw how you handled that monster!" NaHafa said. "That was so brave of you!"

We went back to the creature with a detonator switch and a pack of C4 charger bombs. "This is where we say goodbye to one another," I told the Untouchable. "It was fun, but it ends right here and now."

Slowly and heroically, Nahafa and I walked away from the Untouchable. The armed soldiers surrounding us were ready to fire on the monster as soon as NaHafa and I were out of the line of fire.

"Run! Get back! It is about to explode!" I said, running toward them. When I was far enough away, I pushed the detonator button and watched the Untouchable go up in flames. He was screaming pitifully as it perished like a human being.

Chapter 9

"I am so glad that it is all over!" NaHafa cried with tears of joy.

The flames cooked the Untouchable quickly and the smell of his burning flesh rose up in the air, turning our stomachs.

Chapter 10:
It's Not Over Yet

NaHafa was proud of me, yet I was so tired and had never felt so out of shape. "I wonder what we should do now!" NaHafa asked me.

"Go to Disney World, the Bahamas or something!" I said, relieved. I felt bad for most of the voyage, but now I felt better than I had in years! I was the lowest ranking person on the ship and yet I defeated such an interesting creature! You know, I was never a fan of going to church and believing in Jesus Christ."

"Tevie, what are you talking about? Are you okay?" NaHafa said.

"I am fine, I just feel so blessed to be back on Earth!" I said. "I think a spirit is trying to tell me something!"

"I see, hero!" NaHafa said.

"I think I will give myself over to Christ!" I said with heart.

I was grateful to see my wife and kids again, for my cadets' sons and daughters would never see their moms or dads again. I now had a different outlook on life.

* * * *

NaHafa went on to teach science and freelance as a motivational speaker, telling others about our extraordinary experience in outer space while my family and I attended

Chapter 10

church regularly. Soon, NaHafa started joining us in church and, as we both became more vested in the gospel, we began doing missionary work around the world. The Warsan Center gave us plaques, not only for surviving the voyage, but also for saving the world from the destruction of the Untouchable. At first, there was the BASIC 12, and then there were nine of us, and then seven of us, and then the final four and then just the two of us. NaHafa and me.

All around the world parties to honor us were thrown. "Can you dig all this honor, madam?" I asked NaHafa. "It seems like they are giving me too much praise."

"You are the one who made all this happen, they should be praising you!" she said.

I responded, "Well, you survived that foolishness too, so that makes you a hero, as well!"

"I guess you are right," NaHafa said. "How are we going to celebrate after this?"

"I am celebrating. I am celebrating that I am alive for Christ now!" I said.

"Amen to that, my main man!"

I found a home in Christ, where I felt safe enough to give all my problems over to God.

* * * *

Back in outer space, the Hexapod exploded and the sub-space ship broke free and got away before the blast destroyed it, too. A tracer at the Warsan Center picked it up and wondered who or what was controlling it. They had no way of knowing that the baby Untouchable born from Safoya's corpse had grown up quickly and was now controlling the ship; no way of knowing that an Untouchable was still out there somewhere…

This is the end…. for now.

Printed in the United States
201284BV00001B/1-78/P